SOUTHERN HOSPITALITY

Sally Falcon

A KISMET™ Romance

METEOR PUBLISHING CORPORATION
Bensalem, Pennsylvania

To Cherry Weiner
who believed and helped make it happen

Acknowledgement: To
Janet Berry & the Arkansas Traveler Pro Rally
for all the sweltering days and cold nights
on the control crew.

SALLY FALCON

An avid romance reader since junior high school, Sally didn't try her hand at writing until years later. While busy establishing herself as a librarian, she accepted a dare from a friend to write a romance. She likes to combine the mood of the romantic comedy films of the 1930's and 1940's with settings taken from the eight states where she's lived. Currently, she lives in Arkansas—a transplanted *Yankee*—juggling her two careers.

_____ PROLOGUE _____

"Logan, you have all the compassion of a rabid dog," Preston Herrington stated, his weathered face showing his total disgust with the younger man lounging in the chair on the other side of the mahogany desk.

Logan Winchester Herrington, VI, stared impassively through slate-blue eyes at his uncle. The older man stood silhouetted against the fan-shaped window that framed the snowy skyline of Boston, his double fists on the desk top propping up his frail arms.

Both men had inherited the same whipcord-lean build from Logan Winchester Herrington, V, Logan's grandfather and Preston's father. Logan, however, was still the epitome of the Herrington male—six-foot, one-hundred-seventy pounds, with his aristocratic features tanned and finely lined from battling the sea for recreation over some thirty-six summers. Preston had looked much the same twenty years ago, before too much alcohol, too many cigarettes, and years of gruelling living as a foreign correspondent took their toll. Until recently, the older man could have been dismissed as only mildly dissipated, but in the past two years it was clear his body was wasting away. A virus contracted in a small Argentine village had forced him to retire from field work and take over the helm of the Herrington Publishing Group, whose holdings stretched across the country. Despite his precarious health, Preston's gray eyes still mirrored the mental vitality that ruled the Herrington empire with an iron will, although his brown hair was liberally streaked with grey while Logan's was still golden brown.

"You've been watching Spencer Tracy movies again, haven't you?" Logan returned, arching his straight, dark brown brows in question, not bothering to sit up. He remained with his right ankle resting on his left knee and his elbows propped on the arms of his Windsor chair. Bracing his chin against his clasped fingers, he watched his uncle from beneath drowsy eyelids.

"That poor man's Kennedy drawl won't get you anywhere this time, my boy. Try to at least act like a human being with blood running through your veins instead of a preppy android." The sarcastic words seemed to drain the normally affable man of his last reserve of energy, and he lowered himself into the green leather chair behind him. He leaned his gray head back, dragging an unsteady hand through his thinning hair. "I held back when you laid into Hyde-White over his latest articles, and when you didn't have enough emotion in you to understand Libby Vaughn's problems during her separation. Today, however, you made me ashamed to call you a relative, much less my heir."

Logan still didn't move, although he'd had to suppress the urge to come to the older man's aid when he sat down. Preston never tolerated anyone drawing attention to his weakness, except his wife, Babs. "You're referring to Reinman's request for time off?"

"Yes, time off to spend at the hospital with his family," Preston answered in confirmation, his anger clear in the rigid lines of his face. "His son is having a kidney transplant. Anyone with the merest hint of feeling wouldn't have cared that the man was already over extended in time off. Some might even be willing to allow the man the time with pay."

"We have company policies, and as office manager I'm expected to see that we follow those policies," Logan replied without moderating his drawl. "You and grandfather created the policies; I simply act upon them."

"You enforce them with all the finesse of Captain Bligh, even your mother has more diplomacy," his uncle stated, closing his eyes for a moment. "That is why I have come to a decision that hasn't been easy. I met with Will Daniels yesterday."

"What does your personal lawyer have to do with publishing magazines?" For the first time Logan was curious. Preston had become overly sensitive since his illness had been diagnosed as viral hepatitis, which made Logan ignore the comment about his mother. Preston usually didn't mention his disdain for his younger brother's widow. The older man's mood swings worried both his wife and his nephew, although neither spoke of it.

"My lawyer came to draw up what is known as a living codicil," Preston continued, a smile that was almost a smirk curving his thin mouth.

"A living codicil? Surely, you're not going to actually threaten me with disinheritance in the hope that I'll curb my evil ways by use of a questionable legal device?"

"We both know that the old goat, my revered father, left his property tied up in a trust for his heirs, since he didn't think any of us would amount to a plug nickel, and he didn't want your mother to have a penny," his uncle replied, but his strange smile remained in place. "This is a stipulation that must be fulfilled for you to receive the full benefit of the Herrington holdings when

I go. You are the last of the line, and I refuse to leave you in control with your present attitude toward life. At best, the doctor says I have five years now that I've been receiving proper medical attention for this bug. In that time, I intend to see you develop emotionally before you become a frozen, humorless replica of your mother with no hope for redemption. I blame myself since I should have returned home twenty years ago when your father died, and not waited until I was forced to by illness.''

"What, pray tell, is going to bring about my salvation? Forty hours of Disney movies? Enforced reading of morality tales?'' He could stoop to the ridiculous if Preston was going to be melodramatic. Illness had made the older man change his attitudes a great deal, though he'd never approved of his sister-in-law's preoccupation with social standing and rigid adherence to "proper behavior.'' Usually Preston was delivering a running monologue on his misspent youth, or on his regret at not marrying his precious Babs until six years ago, Logan remembered with fondness.

"Three months in Arkansas.''

The room became very still as the words echoed off the walnut panelling. Steel-gray eyes bored into the startled blue gaze of the younger man. The office staff would have been amazed if they could see "Logan Legree''—as they called him—sitting bolt upright, his mouth hanging open. Enid Macomb Herrington, Logan's mother, would have been appalled as well. Only Preston knew that the younger man was capable of any expression other than boredom.

"Arkansas?'' Logan finally managed, losing the exaggerated New England accent that Preston hated.

"Yes, it's a state in the South, between Missouri and Louisiana,'' his uncle informed him politely, leaning forward to rest his arms on his desk. His eyes were bright with barely contained emotion.

Logan eyed him suspiciously and carefully sat forward himself, propping his forearms on his thighs. "There's more, isn't there? What am I going to be doing in Arkansas?"

"You're going back to reporting again, but not that highbrow tripe you did for *Art Forum*, or that lofty commentary for *Political Scene*." Preston paused, tightly lacing his fingers together as if to keep from rubbing his palms in glee. "If I'm right, I think you might even get dirty and learn there are sports besides polo, sailing, squash, and rowing."

Logan knew he was gaping again. Writing and sports meant only one thing to the Herrington group—car racing. Racing that wasn't Formula One or even contained to a track. This meant SCCA pro rallies, and crazy men who drove on dirt roads; one step above demolition derbies as far as he was concerned. But why Arkansas, a state where he wasn't sure they spoke recognizable English? The *Rally Driver* was a national publication.

"You're going to Arkansas for human interest stories, and because that's where your guardian lives," Preston answered the younger man's silent question, adding mind reading to his talents.

"Guardian?" Logan shot up out of his chair as he yelled the word in a roar that anyone who had ever worked for his grandfather would have recognized immediately. "You're insane. This virus has affected your mind."

"You haven't only become a man without emotions, Logan, you have also become what a hapless politician called the press at one time—an effete snob," returned his tormentor, showing no signs of madness, or even anger. "You'll be under the guidance of T.L. Planchet to learn some humility and hopefully get back some feelings that I know you had at one time. There is life beyond Boston, my boy."

"And if I refuse?" Logan leaned over the desk in much the same manner Preston had just minutes before. The low snarl would have intimidated others, but not a Herrington—both men knew it.

"If you refuse, the Herrington trust will be in Babs's care when I die. You'll have a moderate allowance, no position in the Herrington group, and the total assets will go to charity eventually."

"So, if I want to be part of the Herrington group's future, I exile myself to some godforsaken spot and play out your Victorian morality lesson?" Logan didn't bother to hide his distaste at the prospect. Three months in a cultural wasteland—no symphony, no ballet, no theater—with people who listened to music that extolled the virtue of loving their trucks.

"Yes, and you had better be more humble Oliver Twist than spoiled Little Lord Fauntleroy, or the second part of the codicil goes into effect," Preston explained, now grinning from ear to ear with a smile that would have put the Cheshire Cat to shame.

Logan swore again and kicked the finely crafted mahogany desk that had been in the Herrington family for over two centuries. His angular face was flushed in anger, and his hands doubled into tight fists. Staring at his uncle's face, he was half-tempted to strike the man that he loved above anyone else in the world, unaware that he was showing the first honest emotion Preston had seen from him in two years.

ONE

"Oh, Daddy, what have you done to me this time?" Tory Planchet murmured under her breath as she surreptitiously peered over the top of her sunglasses. The subject of her scrutiny was the man coming out the door of the Little Rock Airport terminal.

Of course this was her passenger, but Logan Herrington wasn't what she'd expected. But the rest of the day had been a disaster, so it fit. Why *shouldn't* he be broad shouldered, lean hipped, and have the most gorgeous head of thick, golden-brown hair she'd ever seen? She'd been expecting stooped shoulders, a bow tie, and visible signs of too much inbreeding.

Her morning had been spent hanging wallpaper with her sister-in-law, aided by a six-year-old child chewing gum and a three-year-old with a lollipop. Then Tyrone Lucius Planchet called to commandeer his only daughter's services as chauffeur for the reporter from *Rally Driver*. When T.L. said jump, he expected everyone to say, "How high?"—even his obstinate daughter. The fact that she was hot and sweaty, hadn't yet eaten lunch, and the plane was landing as he spoke didn't matter.

13

T.L. wanted her at the airport pronto to pick up "my old friend Pres's boy, who has come South for his health."

She should have been suspicious; that old fox T.L. wasn't to be trusted. Tory knew the man leaving the baggage area had to be Herrington, although *boy* was stretching it. He had at least five years to her own thirty. He had to be Herrington because he had Yankee stamped all over him. She'd have recognized the signs even if she hadn't spent her freshman year of college in New York. *Who else would be carrying an overcoat and wearing a wool sports jacket in April?*, she asked herself as he shrugged out of his gray tweed jacket. She gulped when he slung the garment casually over his shoulder, holding it in place with his index finger. The action pulled his brown shirt taut over his chest, his very nice chest.

No, she wouldn't be distracted. She had a right to sulk about this chore. Leaning back, she rested her elbows against the window frame of her truck and propped one sneaker-clad foot on the running board. She hoped she looked nonchalant. Mr. Logan What's-it Herrington didn't look like he was any happier to be here than she was, no matter what number came after his name. He could save his complaints for T.L. and her brother, Curtiss, the rally coordinator. She'd been pushed around enough for one day, and it was barely two o'clock.

Her daddy was going to pay for this, the old scala-wag, she vowed, blowing a very proficient bubble with the gum her nephew had given her. T.L. even had her calling him names as "good-ole boy" after his drawling, laid-back instructions on the phone.

Logan scanned the half dozen cars that lined the curb, his eyes drawn immediately to the vintage Ford truck and the young woman leaning against it. In spite of her juvenile pursuit of blowing bubbles, she was definitely a woman. No teenager could fill out those stone-washed jeans or the white cotton camisole as well. He wondered if her face was as tantalizing as her slender but gently curved figure. Somewhere he'd read that women with pear-shaped figures were the most sensual. Nicely rounded hips and breasts gave her a feminine grace despite the baseball cap that was pulled low over her forehead.

She looked straight ahead with no indication on her heart-shaped face that she knew he was intently studying her profile. Her hair was a rich, dark brown, almost black, where her pony tail was threaded through the back of her cap. Oversized sunglasses were perched on her straight nose and her mouth was tempting as she licked her lips after completing her bubble.

Logan shook his head to dismiss his errant thoughts and loosened the knot of his charcoal-colored knit tie. He had to find Planchet, not ogle the local scenery. The heat was getting to him already. There was a thirty degree jump in temperature from cool, crisp Boston to sunny and seventy Little Rock as the pilot had cheerfully announced just before landing. Well, he'd take overcast and cold any day, if his *guardian* couldn't bother to be on time. He'd heard southerners had a slower paced life, but the plane had been on the ground for a half hour.

Looking around, he grimaced when he realized that everyone else was gone. Only a hotel van and the Ford truck remained with any sign of human life. A line of empty cars were parked to his left at the airline arrivals. No one seemed to care, however. Actually, there didn't seem to be *anyone* around to care, he amended in surprise. The unusual solitude around the airport added to his sense of unreality. There weren't a multitude of honking horns from bumper-to-bumper cars jockeying for position that drowned out the police whistles to keep the traffic moving, and there wasn't a taxi in sight.

With a sigh of resignation, he picked up his suitcase, cursing the overcoat he wouldn't need. "Excuse me, can you tell me how far it is to the city?"

"Sir?"

Her soft question was almost too studied, Logan thought, narrowing his eyes. Unfortunately, her sunglasses masked her expression, so he couldn't tell if she was really startled by his approach. "Are you waiting for me?" he asked bluntly, fairly sure he already knew the answer.

"I beg your pardon?" She drew herself up to stand straight, her head level with his shoulder.

Logan had an impulse to laugh. She had more of a regal stance than a half dozen debutantes who were registered in the Blue Book. No, he corrected himself when her nose tipped upward. She was stiffening up more in the dowager class, rivaling his own mother's impervious stance.

"My plane just arrived and you seem to be waiting for someone. Could I be the person you're picking up?" he continued. He knew he was being cryptic, but he couldn't seem to resist. For some reason, he wanted to see what it would take to get her to remove her sunglasses.

She put her hands on her hips with emphasis and looked him up and down. Logan had the impression she didn't like what she saw. The emotion, however, could be an extension of the discontent he'd been feeling since Preston made his ultimatum, and the resulting confrontation between his mother and his uncle.

Tory had to admit that Logan Herrington was even more impressive close up, and that she was also behaving very badly. Part of it was Herrington's fault, though, with his very upper crust accent and demanding tone of voice, even if there was an interesting, smokey quality to it. She was already mad at T.L., so she didn't need to be patronized on top of it. And he didn't have to have such an aloof look in his gray-blue eyes or glare down his solid Roman nose.

"Sir, I think you're mistake—"

"Ma'am, is this fella bothering you?"

Both Tory and Logan were surprised by the interruption. The policeman had come up quietly, seeming to appear out of nowhere.

"Look, officer, there's been a misunderstanding," Logan stated, giving his companion an accusing look.

"I was addressing the young lady, sir, if you don't mind," the policeman reprimanded, losing his affable smile.

"No, sir, there's no problem here. This gentleman is looking for his ride," Tory put in with a small twinge of remorse. She had to make up ground fast. Her temper had only made a silly situation worse. *Dumb move, Victoria.* "I think he was expecting my daddy instead of me. I'm Tory Planchet."

"You're old T.L.'s girl? Well, I'll be. My boy played ball with your brother at A.S.U.," the middle-aged officer said with a proud smile. "You tell Trev that Grady King said hi."

"Sure will, Officer King," Tory replied, letting the excess air out of her lungs in a rush of relief. T.L.'s name had done it's usual, and she had the added bonus of the man knowing her brother. Then she looked at Logan.

His straight, dark brows were drawn together over the bridge of his nose. The set of his square jaw had his wide mouth pulled into a grim line. She noticed that there were tiny laugh lines around his eyes and wondered when in the distant past he'd smiled or laughed.

"Ummm, toss your suitcase in the back, and we'll go," she said with an airy wave of her hand, trying to pretend the last few minutes hadn't happened.

When he didn't move, she hesitated. She pulled her sunglasses halfway down her nose and gave him an assessing look once again. "You *are* Logan Herrington, aren't you?"

"Uh-huh," he answered, giving her the impression he'd like to deny it. Without another word he tossed his kid leather case, along with his sport coat and cashmere topcoat, into the back of the truck. He only flinched slightly as he noticed the bits of straw and dirt in the truck bed.

Tory marched around the bulky front end of the truck. She jerked open her door, ignoring the protest of the hinges. Curtiss had driven the truck last, which meant she needed to spend time making up for his neglect. If it didn't have four legs, an object wasn't worth her younger brother's attention, even one of T.L.'s vintage vehicles. Too bad Logan only had two legs, or she could hand him over to Curtiss; however, she'd agreed to be press officer for the rally group. T.L.'s high-handedness, Curtiss's neglect, and her own stupidity were making this a *wonderful* afternoon. And the fact that in spite of his good looks, Logan Herrington's personality almost had less charm than her boorish oldest brother Sanders.

She barely gave Herrington time to get settled before she slammed the truck into gear. Her raw feelings found solace in controlling the modified engine under the pickup's hood. Influenced by her temper, she aimed the truck out of the airport drive with less than her usual skill. Maneuvering the vehicle kept her from admitting most of her present troubles were her own fault, and that Logan Herrington made the truck's cab seem to shrink to half its size.

"Is the airport always this hectic?" her passenger asked, his tone colored with a superiority managed only by inhabitants of metropolitan areas with populations over a million.

"It's never really crowded, Mr. Herrington," she snapped, making the turn onto the road as sharp as possible when the man failed to mask his snort of disdain. "It was planned that way. Unlike a few well-known, congested airports I've been in, this one has the parking traffic separated from the drive-through traffic. That's what gets the airport emptied so quickly—careful planning."

"I see," Logan responded, then fell silent. Tory was sure he was planning his next negative comment while she accelerated down the road toward the expressway. She couldn't very well tell him to stick it in his ear, as if he were one of her brothers.

She gave him a sidelong look, slowing for the entrance ramp. He even had an irritating posture-perfect way of sitting. He certainly didn't look happy to be here, or maybe he was just naturally disagreeable. His air of sophistication didn't mean he wasn't interested in rally racing. She'd learned during her first weekend working on a rally that the conversation could range from Art Deco architecture to yacht racing, as well as driving tactics. Looks meant nothing.

Today no one would guess she was Victoria Planchet, the owner and creator of Bill of Fare Catering, soon to be Bill of Fare Shoppes. She didn't appear to be the same business woman who was a Cordon Blue chef, the recipient of numerous rave reviews from food critics, and winner of many cooking awards. No one would recognize her as the same elegant woman who had accepted the Little Rock Chamber of Commerce's top award just two weeks ago.

"So, how far was the airport planned from your

thriving metropolis, Ms. Planchet?'' Logan asked with irritation, ruining the softening of his companion's mood brought on by her own thoughts.

"You'll see it after we get through the woods and the swamp," she returned, her sweet voice one that would have made Blanche DuBois envious. The wooded scenery on either side of the highway helped her exaggeration, not revealing that they were only a few miles from a city with close to 200,000 people. *He was expecting uncivilized surroundings, so why not give them to him?* she thought, already forgetting her earlier twinge of remorse.

"How fascinating," he replied, his bored tone only confirming her suspicions.

That goaded her into her next move. Deftly she flipped the tape out of the tapeplayer and reached down into the container on the seat between them. A quick glance at the new tape's title she'd selected from her brother's section made her smile in satisfaction. Herrington didn't need to know she was replacing David Sanborn's sax with David Allen Coe. Curtiss's taste for country-western music would add just the right atmosphere to the remainder of the ride. She knew she guessed correctly when her passenger winced the moment Coe began his ultimate country western song, *You Never Even Called Me By My Name*, that included trucks, trains, prison, booze, lost love, and his mama in the appropriate plaintive voice.

"Curtiss says you're here for three months to get human interest material, as well as cover the rallies around the area," Tory began as the city's skyline came into view, her tone suggesting he wouldn't know a human's interest if he fell over it. She forged on, determined that he wouldn't be the only one making keen observations. "From my year at Vassar, let me guess at your background."

"You went to Vassar in New York?" Logan asked, clearly unable to stop himself. His startled question implied she'd just landed from Mars and wanted to see his leader.

"Is there another one? I didn't realize," she returned, smiling placidly while turning off the expressway. "As I was saying, you must have started at Choate, and like all good, little Massachusetts Ivy Leaguers gone on to Harvard."

"Princeton, actually. Herrington's don't like to follow the masses," her companion confided. Tory caught the faint ghost of a smile on his lips out of the corner of her eye, but decided it was her imagination.

"How daring. Princeton it is then, before you followed faithfully in your daddy's footsteps in the family business," she finished in triumph. He couldn't deny he'd joined the Herrington Publishing Group since that was who had sent him here. The touch of humor—no matter how fleeting—almost threw her. There couldn't be too much humor in anyone who said, *awk-too-ally*.

"Only a year at Vassar? Was it the snow?"

There it was again, that hint of amusement in his voice—a voice that was getting a suspiciously heavier New England accent with every syllable. "I only agreed to go North for a year to my mother's alma mater. Then I was allowed to go to the school of my choice."

"Which was?" he prompted, showing real curiosity at what school she selected over Vassar.

"The University of Nevada at Las Vegas," Tory announced proudly with her own touch of superiority before changing gears to scale the steep incline of Cantrell Hill. Herrington wouldn't guess she'd gone to Nevada to learn hotel management, but became so fascinated with catering and food preparation that she'd developed those special skills. Even T.L. was proud of her select catering service that customer demand was now expanding into three retail stores, specializing in meals for what Trevor called the "Zap and Serve" crowd.

"That's certainly an interesting choice," Logan replied without bothering to hide his skepticism.

"The climate was so much better for my health, and I didn't hear how funny I talked three times a day from absolute strangers, who had a distinctive accent of their own," Tory informed him. She knew she was baiting him, but she just couldn't seem to help herself. Although she'd made a number of good friends at Vassar, there were also many who treated her as if she'd just learned to wear shoes and eat food with utensils.

She wasn't sure if that was why she was being so hateful to Logan, or if it was his similarity to her oldest brother. Sanders tolerated his younger sister and two brothers, but was always critical of anything they said or did. Tory, Trevor, and Curtiss were sure that T.L. had been given the wrong baby at the hospital and got Sanders by mistake. Of course, Sanders wasn't anywhere near as good-looking as Logan.

As quickly as the thought came, Tory knew she needed to do something to offset it. "So, was I right, Mr. Herrington? Are you Mr. Ivy League?"

"I get the impression you're describing something that crawled out from under a rock," Logan answered softly, all traces of humor gone from his voice and handsome face.

Tory knew he gave her a searching look from beneath half-closed eyelids before he turned back to watching the houses they passed. "Let's just say the axiom of East meeting West goes tenfold for me with North and South. The cold climate seems to have a decidedly adverse effect on Yankee development."

The silence in the truck's cab was eloquent as Tory

downshifted for a red light. Her hand squeezed the knob of the gearshift tightly as she wondered if she'd gone a tad too far.

"Well, what now, Miz Scarlet?" inquired Logan, his imitation of her own slight accent coming out with the usual disastrous results when a Yankee attempted a southern drawl of any kind.

His mimicry grated on her nerves, even without his name calling. She'd give him a little southern lady's piece of her mind. She snapped her head around to glare at him, whipping off her sunglasses to allow him the full impact of her venomous stare. Her eyes locked with the direct, slate-blue gaze that was much closer than she expected. She wasn't prepared for the tingle of excitement that skated down her spine. Blinking rapidly she tried to maintain her composure, as well as remember her own name under his mesmerizing gaze. The man was lethal, in spite of the last twenty minutes of aggravation he'd caused. He also knew the effect he was having on her from the way his mouth was beginning to turn up on one side. She had to get him home, fast, before she did something utterly ridiculous, such as test what it would be like to kiss his square-cut lower lip.

An irate honk from the car behind them saved Tory from any foolishness. *What am I doing*? she asked herself, steering the truck through the intersection. *I almost made a pass at this infuriating man. If he was what I'd expected, a little weasel of man in a bow tie, I'd have pushed him out of the truck before we reached the city limits.*

Neither of them attempted to break the less than companionable silence as Tory drove through the select subdivision that covered the northern heights above the Arkansas River. As they passed the sprawling ranch-style homes and modern Colonials, Tory tried to figure out why Logan was here. There wasn't a doubt in her mind that Logan didn't want to be here, any more than she wanted him here. When the iron fence that marked the beginning of the Planchet property came into sight, she determined it was time to do a little more probing.

"You'll be staying at the big house with T.L. The property has been in the family since the first Planchet came up from Louisiana, and we've kept several acres up here tucked among the suburbanites. The house was built in the 1890's, as well as the cottage I live in," she said in a rush while punching in the security code on the panel. The gate in front of them glided open the minute she touched the final digit. "Although I suppose Curtiss is officially your host."

"Curtiss is the rally coordinator for the Arkansas Traveler group, right?"

"Yes. You'll be meeting the entire family at dinner tonight," she said, aware that he'd turned to watch her. "Trevor oversees the control crews as the rally master."

"What do they do?"

"The control crew?" Tory took her eyes from the narrow drive for a moment in her astonishment at his lack of knowledge. Logan met her glance without blinking, giving her an almost indiscernible nod as if he regretted his question. "The control crew times each stage of the race. Do you have any idea what I'm talking about?"

Logan moved his head from side to side twice. His shoulders had a rigid set to them, almost as though he was bracing himself for her next words. Tory was completely flummoxed. "Have you ever been to a rally?"

"No. The closest I've gotten has been watching a few European events on ESPN and picking up a copy of *Rally Driver*," Logan answered, giving her a sheepish look that reminded her of her nephew, Ty Daniel.

"But—" Tory never formed her question as the elegant facade of her family home came into view. Her usual feeling of warmth at the sight of the double turreted, forest-green Queen-Anne-style Victorian house was absent. The cause for her disgust was framed in the moon-gate arch of the porch that curved around the house. She should have known that T.L. had something up his sleeve.

If T.L. hadn't gone into business, he'd probably have made a fortune on the stage. Her daddy was one of the biggest hams she'd ever seen, and he loved to play any role that struck his fancy. One day he'd be the serious, hard-nosed business executive—silk three-piece suit and wing tips—and the next it was overalls and a baseball cap. He also had the talent for selecting the character that would irritate the people he was dealing with the most. He loved to keep everyone off balance while he choreographed every move.

She almost felt sorry for Logan, unless his uncle had given him fair warning ahead of time. She doubted it. T.L. was something that had to be experienced, and Logan was about to do just that. With his disgruntled mood over being in Little Rock, Logan was a lamb going to slaughter, and she was delivering him to the packing house.

As Tory suddenly braked to a stop, Logan wondered what caused the look of horror in her maple-colored eyes—eyes that had fascinated him from the moment she took off her sunglasses. Although he much preferred the view that was limited to Tory's profile, he turned his head to see what caused her alarm.

A man of about sixty sat contentedly rocking in a chair that was perfectly framed by the graceful lines of the porch entrance. He wasn't hard to miss because he stood out like a sore thumb against the backdrop of the stately house. Logan was more familiar with Colonial and Federal architecture, but he recognized the Planchet house as a showpiece of its period. A glowing example that didn't need a man dressed in dirty jeans, a thread-bare shirt, and gaudy suspenders marring its splendor.

With a feeling of dread, Logan knew who the man with the litter of empty beer cans at his feet was. "Is that your father?"

"Yup, that's my *Paw*," Tory replied through clenched teeth.

Logan noticed her lilting voice suddenly had a flat, nasal quality. He gave her a sharp look, but she was already scrambling out of the truck, shutting her door with a slam.

"Well, girl, what took ya so darn long?" T.L. bel-lowed from the porch as his daughter ate up the ground between them in a straight legged stride. "T'ain't hardly anyplace further away than a twenty minute jaunt from here."

Logan got out of the truck cautiously, his eyes never leaving the pair who were now eye to eye on the porch. He couldn't hear Tory's reply because she didn't attain T.L.'s decibel level. As the two continued their heated discussion, Logan pulled his suitcase and coats out of the back of the truck. As he shook out his coat and jacket, he wondered if Preston would allow him to stay at a hotel during his stay, or even take a temporary apartment. With one twanging sentence, the broad-faced T.L. Planchet had set his teeth on edge. Given three months of the man, Logan knew he would undoubtedly leap off the overhang where the ground fell away on the far side of the house.

"Well, Mr. Herrington, how was yer trip?" T.L. asked anyone within twenty miles as Logan placed his foot on the first step of the porch.

"Fine, sir, just fine," Logan murmured, ascending

the seven wooden steps that brought him level with the others. Reluctantly, he put down his suitcase to clasp the hand T.L. stuck out. While Logan had his entire arm pumped by the older man, he looked toward Tory for some help. She stared back at him blandly, only raising her eyebrows in mild inquiry. Her expression gave nothing away as she rocked back and forth from the heels to the balls of her feet, her hands clasped behind her back.

Logan's shoulder was saved from being dislocated by a feminine voice from behind the wood-framed screen door. "T.L., is that your company?"

"Sure is, Arnette. Come on out and meet Pres's boy," T.L. bellowed over his shoulder and released his death grip on Logan's hand.

Rapid footsteps on a bare wood floor were the only answer to the summons. A slender woman close to T.L.'s age appeared in the doorway. Logan almost heaved a sigh of relief at her appearance as she opened the door. She was dressed in a casual cotton dress of a delicate rose color with an apron in a complimentary, tiny-figured design tied around her waist. Her blond hair was lightly streaked with gray and pulled into a demure bun.

"T.L., why are ya'll standing out here on the porch?" Arnette demanded in a gentle but firm voice, placing her hands on her hips. "What will Mr. Herrington think of our manners, especially with this mess I told you to clean up still here?"

"Now, Arnette—"

"Don't try to sweet talk, Tyrone Lucius," the lady interrupted, actually admonishing him by shaking one finger at him. The action reminded Logan of Babs scolding Preston for overworking. "I told you I wanted this house spotless with company coming, and the whole family descending on us for dinner. You have no more

sense than little Ty Daniel. Now, introduce me to this
nice young man.''

"Arnette Montgomery, this is Logan Herrington, our
guest for the next three months," T.L. said immediately, his voice lowering to a reasonable level. "Arnette
is my very own benevolent despot, boy. She's taken
care of this household for almost twenty years.''

"A pleasure to meet you, Ms. Montgomery," Logan responded, trying to suppress a smile at T.L.'s
cowed expression. His uncle looked the same after one
of Babs's lectures, and his aunt usually had the same
amused gleam of triumph in her eyes as the lady who
now graciously shook his hand.

"You call me Arnette, just like your uncle Pres
does," she said quietly, giving the two Planchets that
flanked her a derisive look. "At least I can be assured
of a real gentleman with manners to appreciate my work
in the next few months. Any relative of Preston
Herrington's knows how to behave.''

"What room have you prepared for Logan, Arnette?"
Tory broke in before Logan could ask just when the
older woman had met his uncle. This was the first he'd
heard that Preston had ever been in Arkansas.

"I put him in Trev's old room in the east turret,"
Arnette answered, then glanced at her watch. "Tory,
you get Logan settled, then get dressed in something
presentable for dinner. T.L., you pick up those cans
like I told you, or you can find your dinner out at
Curtiss's stable with his horses. Excuse me now, Logan, I have a cake to get in the oven.''

She marched back into the house without another
word. Logan picked up his suitcase, looking expectantly at Tory to lead him to his room. After Arnette's
departing orders, he was in no doubt about who was the
boss. T.L. was already bending his stocky frame to
clean up his beer cans.

"This way, Logan," Tory muttered, jerking her head in the direction of the screen door. She spun around on one heel with a squeak of her sneaker before he could answer. With a nod to T.L., Logan obediently followed. He wasn't sure what to expect on the other side of the door, but he knew his visit to Arkansas wasn't going to be as boring as he had anticipated.

TWO

Logan didn't try to keep up with Tory's brisk pace along the hallway that stretched through the middle of the house. The view of her gently swaying hips needed to be appreciated from a distance. Although his attention was centered on Tory, he had an impression of the rooms they passed. Arnette was humming in the kitchen just inside the back door, and there were brief glimpses of rooms with heavy, ornate furniture, and vivid colors through open archways. The rug beneath his feet in the hall and on the stairs wasn't new, but was a high quality Turkish style that he knew was well cared for and expensive. All around him was the pleasant smell of lemon oil from the gleaming woodwork.

Tory disappeared through the first door at the top of the stairs. Logan regretted that they'd reached their destination so quickly; and it wasn't just because he couldn't watch her enticing figure unobserved any longer. He strongly suspected this would be his last chance to be alone with Tory, if she had her way. Her heart-shaped face had been devoid of expression since he'd admitted knowing nothing about rally racing. He wasn't, however, about to explain the reason for his uncle's assignment. He could imagine the look of disdain he'd receive from the lady.

Tapping one foot, Tory was standing in the middle of the room with her arms crossed below her breasts. No, he wasn't about to explain until he'd been here a little longer, and he'd gotten to know Tory much better. Right now, his intentions of friendship seemed ludicrous with Tory standing next to the huge sleigh bed that seemed to dominate the room. She looked very fragile and delicate surrounded by the rich rosewood furniture and the heavy royal-blue velvet that draped the room from the windows to the half-tester over the bed.

"Well, this is it," she stated in a monotone, her eyes following his quick inspection of the room.

"What?" Logan practically snapped, wondering if she'd been reading his mind. Then he rapidly dismissed the thought. She couldn't know he'd been picturing her in the lace frippery that Victorian ladies always wore beneath their somber gowns, playing chaste maid to his urbane, but licentious, gentleman.

"This is your room. I hope you find it comfortable, even though it used to give Trev nightmares when he was younger," she explained while giving him a considering look. "T.L. is into the heavier and more ornate the furniture, the better. I confiscated most of the Duncan Phyfe and Hepplewhite when I moved to the cottage."

"Where is the cottage exactly?" Logan asked in a bid to keep her talking and in the room. He tossed his belongings onto the satin brocade bedspread without a second thought.

"It's just a stone's throw from the house. I think you can see it from here." She turned to the window nearest her. "Yes, you can see the top of the roof from here."

Logan went to stand behind her, looking over her

slender shoulder to where she was pointing. Ignoring the delicious smell of jasmine that clung to Tory, he concentrated on the lawn that stretched out to a stand of oak trees where two turrets peaked out from the budding foliage. "It's a replica of the house?"

"Yes, only it's a single story instead of three. My great-great grandfather built it for his mother-in-law, sort of a dower house," she confirmed, turning as she spoke. Her startled expression told Logan she hadn't known he was so close. Involuntarily her hands came to rest on his shoulders to keep from tumbling backward onto the window seat.

Logan was willing to oblige and placed his own hands lightly at her waist. All he wanted to do was kiss her, but by the expression on Tory's lovely face—once she'd gotten over her surprise—all she wanted to do was hit him.

"I have to go now," she said, her voice low and husky with a slight catch in it. She swallowed quickly, wetting her lips and giving him an almost beseeching look.

"Why so soon? I thought the conversation was just getting interesting." Logan tried to look as innocent as possible, although the aching that was beginning to take hold of his body was anything but. His hands tightening against the gentle curve of her waist when she started to step away also belied his words. "Would you like me to apologize now or later?"

"Apologize for what?" she returned, remaining motionless as she blinked up at him, her maple-brown eyes widening in confusion.

"Apologize for whatever I've done that has you treating me like yesterday's trash, or for something I'm about to do," Logan murmured. He couldn't resist raising his hand to tip back her cap for a better view of her face. Neither of them noticed that it fell off, landing silently on the floor.

"There's nothing you need to apologize for except being here, and that won't send you back any sooner," she stated with heat, the soft bewilderment in her eyes quickly changing to indignation. "Now, before you do anything stupid, I suggest you unhand me, or I'll deliver a very well placed kick, Mr. Herrington."

Logan stepped back at once, not because of her threat, but because he knew he'd pushed her too far, too quickly. He turned to the side, sweeping his arm out to point her way to the door. "I'll look forward to seeing you at dinner then, Ms. Planchet."

She left the room without a backward glance. Logan stood where she left him, rubbing the back of his neck with his hand. "Well, I certainly impressed the hell out of her with my smooth approach."

In a very short time he'd become fascinated with Tory Planchet and impatient to know more about her. Who was this woman who drove a mint condition 1938 truck with practiced ease? Did she really go to Las Vegas after a year at Vassar? He didn't have any answers, and he wasn't sure he really cared, except that learning the answers meant spending more time with Tory. Right now, he wanted to know that he'd see her on a regular basis over the next three months. Unfortunately, that prospect seemed very dim at the moment, thanks to his ham-handed pass.

Jerking off his tie, Logan reflected that his dealings with Tory thus far were not going to win him any prizes. His stupid comment about Scarlet O'Hara had been unnecessary and petty, although it accomplished one thing. He'd wanted to know the color of her eyes. But nothing he'd imagined came close to the clear, sparkling gaze—the color of maple syrup—that was framed by black-velvet lashes. She couldn't be called beautiful, and he considered that a compliment. Her expressive face and those wide, brown eyes could make a man promise her anything she wanted. No, there wasn't a thing that the fictional Scarlet could teach Tory. With a single, stunning look, she'd frozen his next sarcastic words in his throat and had him gaping like a fool.

"Uncle Pres will be so pleased with my progress at this point," Logan murmured, dragging his fingers through his thick hair in an absentminded gesture before unbuttoning his shirt. The first person he had encountered, he'd managed to alienate in less than a half hour, a new record even for him.

He shrugged off his shirt, crushing it into a ball without realizing it and tossed it on the bed. It would be a challenge to change Tory's mind about him, but one he was able to meet. A Herrington always got what he went after. He had plenty of time, some ninety days and nights, to change the lady's mind about Yankees. It was the nights that interested him the most, he decided, walking to the window for another glimpse of the cottage. He was confident that before too many nights passed he'd discover just how Tory decorated her bedroom.

The subject of his plans stood on the porch considering her next move. Her own words haunted her all the way down the stairs and out of the house. *I suggest you unhand me? Yuck, yuck, yuck. How melodramatic can you get, Victoria?* Her caustic thoughts kept her from thinking about how tempting it would have been to stay in Logan's room.

"Well, I suppose it was better than an I'm-not-amused—just barely," she muttered, walking to the porch railing. Curtiss was welcome to their newly arrived guest. She would only deal with him during the actual rallies. That meant she only had to worry about turning into an imbecile twice in the next three months.

Looking across the lawn, she considered tracking down another Planchet imbecile, one in jeans and suspenders with razorback hogs running rampant all over them. She spotted him lounging on one of the gazebo benches. He was still in good-ole-boy mode, which meant she wouldn't get anything worthwhile out of him. She'd wait until he changed roles again, dressing himself in pinstripes and smoking his two-fifty cigars. Then she'd find out more about Logan Herrington's visit. She smiled at the prospect as she skipped down the porch steps.

Halfway across the lawn she looked back at the house on impulse and was immediately sorry. Logan was staring down at her from his bedroom window. She couldn't gauge how long he'd been standing there. He had enough time to take off his shirt before pulling aside the patterned sheer curtain that would obstruct his view. It also gave her a clear view of his very nice chest that was now spectacular, his shirt having masked the light covering of golden-brown hair over taut flesh.

Tory swallowed the sudden constriction in her throat, cursing Arnette for swearing by vinegar and newspaper, which made the windows so clear, almost non-existent. She could still feel the warmth of Logan's hands on her waist. Now, she had this enticing picture of his gorgeous chest to carry around in her already confused brain.

Purposely she broke the hold of his slate-blue eyes, turning once more to the haven of her cottage. Work was what she needed to get her mind off her theatrical daddy and the encroaching stranger. She held her head high, her back straight, and walked with a relaxed, measured stride as she thought about calling her contractor to check on whether the marble countertops had arrived. Logan Herrington and his marvelous chest were of little importance to her. She had a business to get off the ground, and couldn't waste time standing around fixating on some overbearing, opinionated, domineering man. She'd already learned the hard way that that type of man wasn't for her, and it certainly didn't mix well with her career. She'd concentrate on getting Bill of Fare Shoppes ready to open, and leave Logan Herrington to the rest of her family.

As Logan looked around the large dining room table at the Planchet family, he could imagine his mother's reaction. She'd approve of Sanders, his wife Adele, and their son Basil—the picture of the successful executive and family—although Enid Macomb Herrington never allowed children at her table. Looking at T.L., who had only added a broad yellow tie with a florescent-green palm tree to his earlier outfit, and the other boisterous Planchets, Logan could hear his mother's words the night before he left Boston.

"Preston, who *are* these people?" she'd asked her brother-in-law who was seated yards away at the far end of the formal dining room. The best Irish linen, sterling silver, and Waterford crystal graced the perfectly appointed table even for a family dinner of four. "You're sending my son off to some godforsaken place to stay with these people we know nothing about."

"I know something about them," Preston returned in a voice as quiet as Enid Herrington's, but it carried easily down the table.

"That is precisely my point, Preston. If you don't mind my being so blunt, you have the judgement of a toad at times," Enid answered, her voice growing even softer, which was sign that she was becoming angry.

"Mother, this really isn't—"

"Not now, Logan," his mother interrupted, waving aside his words with a practiced flip of her hand. "Your uncle and I are discussing this."

Logan lapsed into silence, but almost lost his composure when he glanced at Babs across the table. She was crossing her eyes, giving her opinion of the other woman's behavior.

"Nothing you have to say will change the situation, Enid. Logan's agreed to go on this assignment," Preston stated, tossing his napkin down next to his dessert plate. "Now, I'm feeling slightly fatigued so Babs and I will forego the traditional idle after dinner chitchat."

"Well, I've never—"

"Yes, you have, Enid, a number of times—whenever I've been excessively rude," Preston broke in as he rose cautiously to his feet. "And you undoubtedly will again, since I also have the manners of a toad when it suits me. Just remember one thing, my dear. I alone control H.P.G., so whatever I say goes, goes."

Logan had spent the rest of the evening placating his mother. It hadn't been so much to settle her nerves, but to keep her from taking her anger out on Babs once he was gone. Preston and Enid were constantly at war, although usually an armed truce. When open warfare broke out, it was Babs who always got caught in the middle.

"Logan, hepps," the childish words brought him back to the present, along with a chubby, dimpled hand clutching his sleeve. He turned his attention to the blond-haired, blue-eyed, three-year-old temptress who'd staked her claim on him before dinner.

"Amanda Sue, Mr. Logan is eating his dinner. He doesn't want to help cut up your meat," Tory told her niece gently from where she sat on the other side of the child. She gave Logan an apologetic look over the little girl's head, meeting his gaze for the first time all evening.

"Do too," Amanda Sue insisted, turning her limpid eyes up at Logan by cocking her head to the side and giving him a beseeching look through the fringe of her bangs.

"Of course, he does," Logan agreed, unable to resist that look and hoping to avert a scene. As he went about his task, he surreptitiously watched Tory talking to Curtiss's wife, Leeanne, who had barely said a word all evening.

When Tory stepped into the living room earlier, Logan wasn't sure it was the same woman he'd met that afternoon, but this woman was just as riveting to his senses. She stood framed in the archway, an arrestingly sophisticated figure in a silky paisley cossack blouse and a pencil-slim maroon skirt. Her glossy brown/black hair was down, coming almost to her shoulders with the sides swept back by gold barrettes. She had aimed a haughty look in his direction and gone to greet the rest of her family.

"Oh, for heaven sake, Pooh, leave Curtiss alone," Tory called across the table to her oldest brother. "What you don't know about animals could fill volumes. Let Curtiss handle his own practice."

Sanders sent his sister a scathing look before patting his thin mouth with his napkin. "Victoria Camille, I've told you countless times how irritating that repellant name is. I don't want to remind you again."

Logan felt like an observer at a tennis match as he turned to watch Tory's reaction. Her brilliant smile slammed into his heart at high velocity, although it was actually aimed at her brother. "Yes, I know, dear Pooh, that's why I always remember to use it when you're being your most pompous."

"Now, Piglet, you're stealing my material," Trevor broke in, his grin taking the sting out of his reprimand. Of the three brothers he resembled Tory the most—with the exception of a nose that had been broken at least once. "It was *my* favorite book, and I christened everyone appropriately."

"And created yourself Christopher Robin, the only

human in the book," Curtiss added, shaking his shaggy blond head in disgust.

"You're just mad because you weren't born yet, and I was over that phase by the time you came along," his brother shot back in triumph.

"Now, ya'll, I'm gettin' tired of this bickering. You're all supposed to be adults," T.L. interrupted, giving his grown children a dark look. "What's our company gonna think?"

Later Logan was appalled by what he did next, even though it earned a look of approval from Tory. At T.L.'s question he burst into laughter, suddenly understanding the meaning of the nicknames. Trevor had been a Winnie-the-Pooh fan and gave his family the names of the characters. Pooh lived in the woods under the name of Sanders. The image of the forty-year-old business man dressed in his Brooks Brothers suit with his head stuck in a pot of honey was the ludicrous picture in his mind. His sense of humor overcame his sympathy for the other man's displeasure with his sister.

"I'm sorry, but it suddenly struck me as funny," he explained weakly as all eyes were trained on him. Enid Herrington would send him to his room without any supper for such a gaffe. "Please, tell me some more. I was an only child, so life wasn't terribly exciting as a juvenile."

As Curtiss and Trevor competed to tell the most outrageous story, Logan caught Tory giving him an assessing look. His mother certainly wouldn't approve, but he was beginning to enjoy himself. Arkansas might not be as horrible as he had anticipated. A noisy dinner with the Planchets was a vast improvement over his usual solitary meals at his townhouse. The only thing that would give him more satisfaction would be an intimate dinner for two with Victoria Camille Planchet. He promised himself that pleasure as he turned his head to snare the lady's startled gaze. The becoming stain of rose across her cheeks told him she was all too aware of his thoughts.

"Trev, I want off the rally," Tory said into the black candlestick phone the second her brother answered at his end.

"What? Geez, I just walked in the door," he replied impatiently. "Why didn't you say something at dinner earlier? It's almost midnight."

"Don't you think I know that?" Tory shot back, rolling her eyes at the ceiling. She'd spent the past few hours wondering just what to do about her Herrington situation, and waiting for Trevor to get home so she could settle it. "I started calling you twenty minutes after you went off the air at ten-thirty, Mr. Sportscaster, who always forgets to turn on his answering machine. Where have you been?"

"Out for a drink, not that it's any of your business, little sister." Trevor's voice was amused at her harried demand. "What's this about, wanting to quit the rally staff?"

"You'll have to get someone else to handle the media," Tory said quickly, jumping up from the pale-yellow Grecian couch to pace the length of her living room. She almost regretted her sudden need to break all connection with anything that had to do with Logan Herrington. "There's just too much to do with the shop renovations. I hadn't realized how lousy the timing would be when I agreed to help."

"Look who's talking about lousy timing. You know how hard it is to get people to do the administrative work, and you wait until barely two weeks before—" he broke off suddenly, causing Tory to stop dead in her tracks. She held her breath, cursing her stupidity at calling Trevor instead of Curtiss. There was slim chance he'd take her excuses at face value, but she knew it was a futile wish from the knowing laugh at the other end of the phone line.

"This sudden panic wouldn't have anything to do with our dinner guest, would it? Now that I think about it, you picked him up at the airport today, but you hardly exchanged more than two words with old Logan all during dinner," Trevor exclaimed, highly amused by his observations. "So, what gives? Did the big, bad Yankee give you a hard time?"

"Trevor, get real."

"Well, I think I should know all the details, if I have to defend your honor, or whatever it is I'm supposed to do." His tone was overly sincere, which didn't fool his sister, who knew he hoped she'd become frustrated with his nonsense, then make an incriminating slip. Tory smiled to herself, since nothing had actually happened between her and Logan. She decided to quit the rally to insure that nothing would. In less than twelve hours, the man had disturbed her more than any man she'd ever met. It would be best if she could avoid him whenever possible.

"You're weird, you know that?" she asked, forcing herself to give a light laugh. "I've just got too much to do. We have two wedding receptions and a huge retirement party to cater, besides getting the shops ready. Lou Abbott told me today we can probably have our grand opening at Park Plaza two weeks ahead—"

"Ahead of what? What's the matter?"

"I thought I heard someone at the front door." Tory cocked her head to the side and listened for the sound again. She had to be mistaken. No one would be knocking at her door at this time of night. "Good Lord, someone is knocking at the door."

"You've got to be kidding," Trevor challenged, implying that his sister was using it as an excuse to end their conversation at a highly interesting point.

"No, I'm not kidding. Listen." She held the earpiece in the direction of the entrance as the knocking became more insistent. "Hang on a second, there might be something wrong at the main house."

"Victoria, you keep talking to me while you answer the door. That phone cord of yours could stretch all the way downtown, and you don't know who's out there," her brother ordered.

"Honestly, Trev, the gate is secured at night," she returned in exasperation, but she followed his instructions, walking toward the door as she spoke. With presence of mind, she turned on the porch light, leaving the entryway dark. The second she looked out the window that flanked the large oak door, she regretted letting her late-night caller know she was awake. For some unknown reason, Logan Herrington was standing on her doorstep.

"Who is it? Tory?" Trevor's anxious voice broke into her speculative thoughts.

"Ah, it's just Arnette," she answered quickly, too quickly for her brother's sensitive ears.

"Uh-huh, and what does *she* want since you haven't even opened the door?"

"I'll talk to you tomorrow about the rally." She hooked the earpiece into its cradle with Trevor still protesting. Putting the phone down on the hall stand, she toyed with the idea of not answering the door, simply turning off the lights and going to bed. She couldn't give Logan the satisfaction, however, of knowing that she was uneasy about talking to him. Before she could reconsider, she turned the bolt and opened the door.

The phone began ringing before she could say a word. With a sigh of annoyance, she picked up the phone and lifted the earpiece. Knowing it was Trevor, she demanded, "What?"

"Tell me who it is, or I'm dialing 911," he stated, matching her imperious tone.

"All right, it's Logan. Are you happy now? And no, I don't know what he wants because I haven't had a chance to ask him yet," Tory snapped, her impatience rising with every syllable. She cut the connection with a decisive click and turned to glare at the subject of her conversation as she thumped the phone back onto the hall stand. Thanks to Trevor's untimely call, Tory's plan to leave Logan on the doorstep was ruined. He was only a foot away. Meeting her hard stare with slightly raised eyebrows, he closed the door without a word and shut out the light from the porch.

"Remind me not to call on you late at night," he said softly, his voice sounding dark and mysterious in the shadowed entryway.

"Yes, it *is* late," Tory agreed. With what she hoped was a casual move, she took three steps backward into the brightly lit living room. She wondered if Logan would find it strange that she didn't turn her back on him.

"I was taking a walk before turning in and saw your light on," he explained, his steps matching hers. His bland tone and cynical little half-smile told her he knew his explanation was a lie.

"Yes, I, too, always take a walk with what looks like Daddy's Napoleon brandy and two glasses." Defiantly she met his slumberous look—a look as dangerous as a snake's mesmerizing stare. She wouldn't let him know how uncomfortable she felt in her nightshirt for anything in the world. The navy garment hung to her knees and the dark material with its bright logo allowed her to stand with her arms at her sides, seemingly at ease.

"It's an old New England custom to carry something medicinal on a walk, in case of frostbite." His twisted smile turned into a predatory grin before he walked further into the room. In easy strides he moved to the lozenge shaped marble-topped table to put down his offering. "Would you care to join me?" he asked over his shoulder as he opened the bottle. When Tory didn't answer, he turned his head, raising his eyebrows again. "I hate to drink alone."

Tory nodded just to keep him occupied. She had no intention of letting him stay long enough for a companionable drink. Standing her ground, showing no sign of the confused emotions that assailed her whenever Logan was near, she accepted the snifter of amber liquid.

"Well, here's to the 'beginning of a beautiful friendship'," Logan pronounced, lifting his glass expectantly.

Tory stared at him in amazement. He couldn't be serious, showing up on her doorstep in the middle of the night and acting as if he was paying her a friendly call. They'd only met that afternoon, and if she wasn't mistaken, he was quoting the ending line to *Casablanca*. Who was Humphrey Bogart and who was Claude Rains? "What do you want, Logan?"

The only sign of emotion was the telltale tightening of his square jaw before he ambled over and lowered himself into her contour rocker, settling into the powder-blue horsehair upholstery as if he anticipated a long visit. "I thought we should discuss what we're going to do about it," he said quietly, hooking his ankle over his knee.

"About what?" Tory demanded. She had to be dreaming. Logan Herrington wasn't making himself at home in her cottage, issuing enigmatic statements. He couldn't be asking about what she thought he was, could he? Surely he didn't have the same chaotic reaction to her.

"Let's not be coy about this, Tory. We're both mature adults."

"I'm not so sure we both are," she stated, rashly moving toward him. Putting T.L.'s crystal snifter safely on the sewing table next to Logan's chair, she placed her hands on her hips in Arnette's favorite pose. "You have exactly five minutes to start making sense, then you're out of here."

"Victoria Planchet, you're a hard woman," he answered, shaking his head mournfully. "I thought southern women were supposed to be soft, gently-spoken ladies with a kind understanding that was as delicate as a magnolia petal."

"You nipped at Daddy's brandy on the way over here, didn't you?" she inquired, but didn't wait for an answer. "You just ran into one of the fabled steel magnolias, Mr. Herrington. I only deal with mental cases during my optimum functioning hours, which are from eight in the morning to about five in the afternoon. For you, though, it's from noon until five past."

"Tory, you can't deny there's an inexplicable attraction between us. You can't take away the one thing that could make this crazy trip worthwhile," Logan stated, giving her a bewildered look. "Believe me, I don't usually do anything like this, but I've never felt this way about a woman on such a short acquaintance."

She wouldn't let herself think about his last statement. With Logan rising to his feet, she couldn't be distracted from her purpose—getting him out of the cottage before she did something foolhardy. "What do you mean, make this crazy trip worthwhile? Does it have something to do with the fact you know next to nothing about rally racing?"

"Forget about the rally, I want to talk about us." He was standing directly in front of her, getting much too close.

"Why are you here, Logan? You act as though this assignment is some sort of penance you have to pay," Tory countered, trying to ignore the shivers of awareness that raced through her blood. She could feel the heat coming from his body as he took another step closer.

"It isn't important why I'm here, only that we've met, and it's something that can't be ignored." He raised his arms, hesitating a moment when she seemed to shrink away from him. Gently he rested his hands on her stiff shoulders.

"We met just this afternoon. I don't know how you do things in Boston, but in Little Rock, we believe in courtesy—even when strangers test our patience." She was determined not to give into the temptation of his nearness, trying to convince both of them that this was ridiculous. To stay in control, she pressed her point, "Why did Preston Herrington send you to Arkansas?"

Logan had the grace to actually blush at the direct question, but Tory never had a chance to decide if it was from guilt, anger, or frustration. His right hand moved swiftly from her shoulder to snare the nape of her neck, his lips capturing hers in a millisecond of time. Her protest was muffled by his mouth before she could utter a sound.

The kiss took an eternity. Logan seemed to be a starving man, tasting her lips carefully at first as if afraid his long awaited sustenance would disappear like a mirage. Tory was paralyzed by the riot of fireworks that seemed to be exploding inside her head. When she didn't resist, he grew bolder. His tongue licked at the sweetness of her lips before delving within to search for further delight. One of them made a purring sound of approval.

Tory reached out to Logan to keep her balance because the carpet beneath her feet suddenly offered little support, but she found herself grasping empty air. Logan released her as abruptly as he kissed her. She swayed for a moment, attempting to clear her befuddled brain.

"That, Tory Planchet, is what is between us," he said in a clear, concise tone, although she noted he was having trouble steadying his breathing. He ran his hand through his hair in a nervous gesture. "Sleep on that, and I'll get back to you around noon tomorrow."

He walked past her dazed figure, his eyes straight ahead, his step purposeful. The sound of the front door closing with a decisive thud brought Tory to her senses. On unsteady legs, she stumbled to the couch and dropped limply onto the satin covering.

"He has the manners of a Yankee pig, but he certainly knows how to kiss," she muttered, running a hand through her hair in almost the same gesture Logan used minutes before. She'd known he was going to spell trouble from the moment he walked out of the airport terminal, but nothing prepared her for the conflagration that he kindled within her with a simple kiss. No, not a simple kiss. A searing mark of possessiveness that made her want to beg for more and run away to safety as fast as she could—both at the same time.

Sleep on that, he'd said. The arrogance of the man, Tory decided, sitting up abruptly as sanity returned to take a firm hold. She wasn't about to be hornswoggled by any fancy city boy with a fantastic pair of lips. She groaned in despair. Hornswoggled? Her brain was going soft, or she'd been spending too much time around T.L.

She jumped up and headed for the bedroom, determined to get a good night's sleep. Not only did she have to face Logan with a clear head in the morning, she had to take on T.L. There was a reason for Logan being here, besides tormenting her. Tomorrow she was going to find out why.

"Blithering idiot. Blundering fool," Logan muttered under his breath as he crossed the moonlit lawn to the main house. He continued to berate himself as he pulled a battered baseball cap from his back pocket. He'd intended to return Tory's cap during his visit. Of course, that wasn't all he'd intended, but in what seemed to be a continuing pattern, he'd made a hash of the whole thing.

Clutching the cap in his hand, he made himself a promise. He'd find a way to temper his impatience and discover a means to breach Tory Planchet's defenses. He didn't know why it seemed of tantamount importance. He just knew it was, almost as if she held the knowledge of an important secret. Whatever it was, he had to know what was making him behave with such uncharacteristic impetuousness.

There was only one thing he knew for certain. He didn't want Tory to know why he'd been sent here. Around her he felt almost ashamed of his exile, which was ridiculous, but he wanted it kept from her just the same. He'd tell her himself, in his own way, when he judged that the time was right. Certainly not before he saw her brown eyes in passion, soft and darkened to the color of semi-sweet chocolate, her face flushed with excitement.

As he reached the steps to the porch, he ruthlessly erased the tantalizing image that would keep him awake all night. He needed a good night's sleep to deal with this strange situation. Perhaps that was all he needed to release him from his obsession. In the morning, he'd discover that Tory Planchet was just an ordinary woman.

THREE

"Morning, Arnette," Tory announced the moment she walked into the kitchen early the next morning. The wonderful smell of fresh baking filled her senses, but she was here for one reason and wouldn't be side-tracked. "What's the old buzzard up to this morning?"

"Just let me get this last batch out of the oven, hon. You know where the coffee is," Arnette answered with a welcoming smile as she took a tray of warm cookies from the oven.

Tory crossed to the coffee maker under the clear-glass cupboards. She followed the cardinal rule of the kitchen as she poured herself a cup of rich, fresh ground coffee; never bother Arnette when she was in the middle of anything. But when she idly glanced at the cookie sheet that Arnette was deftly balancing, every other thought went out of Tory's head.

"What is T.L. wearing this morning, and why are you making snickerdoodles?" Tory shot out, looking at the sugar-and-cinnamon topped confections with horror. They were T.L.'s traveling snacks.

"If you want to know anything about your daddy,

just march yourself into the dining room, young lady." Arnette didn't bother to look up from her task. "These cookies have to be ready when he is. So, go ask him what you want to know."

Tory turned on her heels, careful not to spill her coffee, and made a beeline for the dining room. The old goat was going to sneak out of town and leave her with Logan without so much as a goodbye. She was brought up short on the kitchen's threshold at the thought of Logan. Spinning around, she said, "Is our resident royalty out of bed yet?"

"If you mean Mr. Herrington, no, he isn't. What have you got against that nice young man?" Her curiosity pulled Arnette's attention away from the cookie sheet to give Tory a searching look.

"You wouldn't understand." She tossed the words over her shoulder, needing to escape the older woman's eagle eyes. As soon as she was out of sight in the hallway, Tory hesitated. She wasn't sure exactly what T.L.'s game was, but it certainly had something to do with the mysterious purpose of Logan's trip, which wasn't to report on any car rally. The most obvious motive of matchmaking simply didn't apply. T.L. wasn't a parent who insisted that marriage was the answer for his offspring, with two of his three marriages ending in divorce. He was pleased that Sanders and Curtiss had started families, but he didn't harangue Trevor or Tory continually about their single status.

She took a deep breath to help collect her thoughts. This had to be handled with a level, cool head. She couldn't let T.L. think she had an inordinate interest in Logan. T.L. didn't need to know that she'd tossed and turned all night long with countless dreams about their visitor. First the disgruntled traveler at the airport, then the nice man that Amanda Sue commandeered as her willing slave, followed by the arrogant, demanding man in her cottage. The most prominent image was Logan stripped to the waist, only he wasn't standing framed in his bedroom window. He was standing at the end of her bed.

The sounds of Arnette bustling around the kitchen behind her brought Tory out of her dangerous memories of the night. It wouldn't do for the other woman to find her daydreaming in the hall. With a deep swallow of Arnette's coffee, Tory headed for the dining room.

T.L. sat in solitary splendor at the head of the long, mahogany table. "Well, darlin', what has you up this early?" he exclaimed in greeting before taking a bite from the ham biscuit in his hand. He was dressed in a subdued brown-and-pale-blue plaid suit that allowed Tory to relax her fixed smile slightly. He was dressed for a fairly rational discussion.

"Seven-thirty seems late, since I'm usually up at five to get the baking started. Even with three months off, I can't seem to shake the habit," she said, slipping into the chair next to him. She refused his silent invitation to share his breakfast, but poured herself more coffee from the Blue Willow coffee pot in the center of the table.

"So, what can I do for you, darlin', or did you come to keep an old man company? I'm sorry to say I have to be at the airport in the next hour and get to Texarkana to avert a drivers' strike."

"You aren't going anywhere until you give me some answers about our guest," Tory said quietly, leaning back in her chair and crossing her legs to show that she had plenty of time. "If you keep to the facts and cut out the histrionics, it shouldn't take more than ten minutes. And you don't need to waste any time by telling me he's here to cover the rallies. The man doesn't like the South *and* has never been to a rally in his life."

T.L. gave her a considering look over the rim of his

coffee cup, a slight smile curving his lips. "That must have been some ride from the airport. Then, again, I didn't raise stupid children."

"Or very patient ones."

"All right, all right. You're just like your mother was when it comes to getting you own way," he answered. He carefully placed his cup in the saucer and leaned forward to rest his forearms on his place mat. "You aren't going to like this, but I don't feel right about telling you all the reasons for Logan's being here. That's between Pres and the boy. If, and when, he wants to tell you, then so be it."

Goaded into a show of temper at being denied such vital information, Tory imprudently challenged T.L.'s decision by giving him some of his own back. "Then it isn't a drug problem? He hasn't been running with a bad crowd, losing heavily at the gambling tables in Atlantic City, and borrowing money from the loan sharks?"

"I guess I deserved that. Are you ready to listen now, or do you have any more flights of fancy?" He gave her a look that was a mixture of sympathy and exasperation, just as he had after her one teenage traffic accident. When she nodded, he continued, "It's nothing unsavory or illegal, so we'll leave it at that. Now that the boy's—"

"Hold it, right there," Tory broke in, putting her hand up for good measure. "From now on, call him Logan, or Herrington, or even Bubba, but please don't call him *the boy*. Even if you did have three sons by different wives, you aren't Ben Cartwright."

"Now that *Logan* is here, we're to treat him like one of the family, and make him welcome."

"You wanted to welcome him by wearing your gardening clothes and laying your accent on with a trowel?" Tory chuckled, thinking about his ratty clothing and

Logan's stunned look the day before. She also knew the old fox had a purpose for doing it, but he wasn't going to share it.

"That was a little lapse on my part," he admitted with an abashed grin. "From now on, we're going to make the b— er, Logan feel at home."

"We are? Just how are *we* going to do this from Texarkana?" Tory asked, giving him enough rope to hang himself. "Logan is still in Yankee dreamland, so I know he isn't going with you."

"I need you to take over as official hostess while I'm gone," T.L. stated, his eyes never leaving her face. "Everyone else is tied up and you've allowed yourself three months off for your remodeling. You can plan your work schedule to suit yourself. Or so you said when Curtiss asked you to help with the rally."

"I feel sorry for the truck drivers in Texarkana," Tory answered tartly, knowing she was trapped, but still trying for some remnant of defense. "Just because Trevor calls me Crusader Rabbit when I get on my soapbox occasionally, doesn't mean I'm a pushover for everyone who needs a favor. I still have a business to run."

"I realize that, but this is a special case. I owe Pres a great deal after all these years. It's the least I could do for the man who introduced me to your mother and put up with me for four years at Princeton. The damned thing is, Tory, Pres is dying."

Tory was stunned by the statement. Preston Herrington was a larger-than-life figure from her childhood memories. His whirlwind visits to and from exotic places had been filled with excitement and thrilling stories. She sat for a moment trying to absorb the news, then one look at T.L.'s sad brown eyes told her that he still hadn't recovered from the shock. This wasn't the time to question him further, so she thought of the one way to put him back to normal.

"I have conditions to this deal. I'll be Logan's hostess whenever you're out of town, if you sign a contract that states you won't interfere with the remodeling or decorating of Bill of Fare Shoppes again—now or at any time in the future."

"I guess we don't come from a long line of horse traders for nothing," T.L. answered with the special sigh parents reserve for times when their children have tried their patience the most. Tory knew it was a sham. His brown eyes were gleaming with approval for the diversion she provided and her crafty proposal. "Though come to think of it, this should be to my advantage. The last time I gave your contractor a little suggestion to improve things, you sent me a hefty bill for the cost of changing it back to the way you wanted it. I'll dictate the contract on the way to the airport and have it delivered to the cottage."

"Fine, we'll shake on the agreement now. I'll have it notarized the first chance I get." She wasn't able to repress her grin of triumph over the deal, jumping to her feet and sticking out her hand. T.L. would never renege once he'd shaken hands on an agreement, but she wanted it in writing just the same.

"Are you sure you don't want to come to work for me? I could use a tough negotiator like you," T.L. asked for the hundredth time as his large hand swallowed hers.

"Yes, because within a half hour I'd come to blows with you or Sanders, probably both. I love you both, but I wouldn't work for two such pig-headed men," she admitted with an apologetic shrug.

"I can see your point. Two Planchets in one office is courting danger, but three could be down right explosive," he murmured. "I'm counting on you to help Logan get settled and that's enough."

More than enough, Tory decided, but kept her skepticism to herself. Something in her expression must have told T.L. she wasn't enchanted with the idea. "Just do your best, darlin'. Now, give your daddy a kiss for luck and beat it."

"You old rogue," she said affectionately as she bent to give him a hug and a kiss on the cheek. "You knew I'd do it, even if you were entertaining Attila the Hun."

He gave a wink and admitted, "You did surprise me with your little bargain, though. I must be getting old."

"I wouldn't lose any sleep over it, you old fox. Remember, I learned from the master." Tory left him to finish his breakfast with a silly grin on his face. She wished she was as happy with the outcome, although it was a godsend that she didn't have to worry about T.L. pestering her contractor any more.

Halfway down the hall to the back door, she realized that she was tiptoeing and looking cautiously back over her shoulder toward the stairway. She called herself ten times a fool for being so apprehensive about meeting Logan. "Oh, get a grip, Victoria," she groaned under her breath as she hurried out the back door with only a quick wave to Arnette. "He's just a very irritating man. You're just off balance because your daily routine has been out of whack since the remodeling started.

"You're also beginning to talk to yourself uncontrollably," she announced as she took the last step to the ground in a disgusted jump.

What was she going to do with him? Most women would be ecstatic at being asked to spend time with a wealthy, eligible man, who wore his clothes well and looked just as good without them. Well, she wasn't most women. She didn't like to be categorized or to put people into categories, even if their square peg seemed custom made for the proverbial round hole. Logan already had the habit of changing shape when she least expected it. Who would he be the next time she saw him?

She headed for the cottage, determined to drag out her appointment book the minute she stepped through the door. If she went through her normal tasks, she'd forget all about Logan Herrington, and whether he would try to kiss her again, or if he would act as if last night never happened. Establishing a routine and sticking to it wouldn't allow her any time to think about a passionate, but obnoxious Yankee. It was so simple, she laughed out loud, almost skipping the rest of the way back to the cottage.

By early afternoon, Tory wasn't as optimistic as she stopped the truck at the back of the house. She turned off the engine and slumped down in the driver's seat. Giving the suit boxes on the seat next to her a morose look, she unfastened her seat belt, but she didn't move.

"A big help my appointment book was," she said softly, allowing her hand to run over the smooth cardboard surface of the top box. Although her day was spent pleasantly, and productively, planning menus for both a wedding and a retirement party, it was the night she was dreading. Tonight she was supposed to attend the Bush's party; a party she would have to invite Logan to because of her promise to T.L. Looking down at the box again, she knew he wasn't going to like what he had to do. What she and her friends found entertaining, he'd undoubtedly find appalling.

Reluctantly, she climbed out of the truck and pulled out the box, holding it in front of her like a shield. She dragged her feet up the steps, dreading what was ahead of her. Under her breath she repeated what she'd been telling herself all afternoon whenever her memory turned traitor at the oddest moments. "He's just a guest of T.L.'s, nothing more, nothing less—a plain, old ordinary friend of the family."

"And that's why I called Mrs. Carter's son, Lloyd,

Logan three times this afternoon,'' she finished in disgust at her rebellious subconscious when she reached the back door. Pulling open the screen door, she stopped halfway across the threshold. The music she heard was coming from the piano, not the radio. None of the Planchets played the piano. T.L. simply bought the grand piano because he adored the cupids and garlands of flowers on the Renaissance piece with the huge cluster columns for legs. Until now, she hadn't thought it was even in tune, but the complex Chopin prelude sounded perfect.

Drawn to the music, she stood quietly in the archway to the double sitting room. His playing was so beautiful she didn't want to interrupt him.

She's here, Logan knew instinctively. The tingling sensation at the base of his spine told him. Resisting the urge to jump up, demanding to know where she'd been all day, he finished the prelude in record time. She couldn't know that he'd spent most of the night lying awake staring at the blue-satin underlining of the half-tester over his bed. Lying awake while he alternately called himself a hormone-crazed fool and imagining Tory tangled in the sheets beside him.

He swiveled away from the mother-of-pearl and tortoise shell keyboard with a little voice inside cautioning him to go slowly. She was standing exactly where he'd first seen her last night. Today she was clutching a large box in front of her instead of carrying Amanda Sue. He drank in the sight of her, wondering how she seemed to fit into the nineteenth century surroundings of the scarlet and yellow drawing room when she was dressed in cotton slacks and a simple blouse. By rights, her curved figure should be covered in lace.

When Tory took a step forward, he nodded cautiously in greeting. He wanted her to set the tone of this meeting. If he was lucky, she would discount his visit to her cottage as a crazy Yankee stunt, and not realize how sincere he'd been. He'd meant every word he'd said, but he also knew it lacked his usual finesse. For now, he'd let Tory take the lead.

"Hello, Mr. Herrington, how's everything going?" Tory asked brightly, stopping abruptly a few feet from him. She seemed slightly apprehensive, her pleasant half-smile not quite reaching her eyes. "You play beautifully. T.L. will be so disappointed he wasn't here. You did know that Daddy was called out of town, didn't you?"

He nodded again without moving a muscle, uncertain whether to stand or remain on the piano stool. Keeping his hands flat on his thighs to keep from reaching for her, he tried to gauge what was happening. Tory was talking to him as if he wasn't much older than her nephews. She stood in front of him, shifting her feet from side to side.

"I see. Well, while Daddy's out of town, he asked me to show you around. If you'd like, some friends of mine are having a party tonight, and they'd be pleased if you'd join us," she went on, not quite looking him in the eye. Her arms tightened around the box making its side bow out. Suddenly her shoulders sagged and she let out her breath by pushing her lower lip forward in the intriguing way she had yesterday. "Look, there isn't an easy way around this. Do you know anything about magic?"

"I beg your pardon?" The strange question forced the words from him in an imitation of his mother's most offended tone. Magic was the last subject he thought would come up. For a half second, he thought Tory was going to turn and walk out of the room without answering.

She gave him an exasperated look, then tossed the box down on the marble-topped table next to her. The cardboard hit the hard surface with a slap that echoed around the quiet room. "This party we're going to tonight has a theme to it. We'll be celebrating Harry Houdini's birthday, so I picked up a costume for you."

"It sounds interesting." He hated costume parties. A bunch of grown people dressed up in ridiculous clothing and acting silly wasn't his idea of a good time. Carefully schooling his features to show only mild inquiry, instead of his abject horror, Logan waited for her to continue.

"It does? Oh, good," she said hesitantly, blinking owlishly at him in surprise while wiping the palms of her hands against her hips. Giving him a guarded look, she suggested, "Why don't you go ahead and try on your costume then. We'll see if it needs any alterations."

It was an effort for Logan to take his eyes from Tory's hands moving against her rounded hips and look at the box. He got to his feet, still trying to show some enthusiasm. *After all*, he reasoned while giving Tory a slight smile, *what can be so bad about a magician's costume? White tie and tails were fairly standard*.

"There's a half-bath under the stairs, so you don't have to go up to your room." Tory's eyes never left his face as his picked up the box.

Logan headed for the hallway, but he was more than tempted to rip the box open then and there. Her agitation wasn't from offering him a starched shirt and cummerbund. *Is this her retaliation for last night? Is the tux some horrible electric blue or blood red?* No matter what, he was going to wear it; whatever her intent. A Herrington never backed down.

Tory almost collapsed onto the scarlet-velvet ottoman the second Logan disappeared into the hall. His unexpected acquiescence had her completely baffled after being prepared for almost anything. The moment he turned away from the piano to stare at her with that unnerving slumberous slate-blue gaze, she almost dropped the box as her knees turned to silly putty. This favor for T.L. was probably going to turn her into a blithering idiot before Logan headed North again.

She knew she should have gotten a regulation tuxedo, but she couldn't resist the temptation of something more contemporary. She was going as Doug Henning, complete with spangled jumpsuit and high-topped sneakers, so David Copperfield had seemed the logical choice. Maybe she should have told him about the magic trick he'd have to perform for his supper and get all the bad news out of the way fast. Last year's party for Bach's birthday would have been a piece of cake for Logan because everyone had to play a minuet. Of course, he wouldn't have liked the knee breeches or powdered wig, she realized, and sat gnawing her lower lip. She should have gotten a tuxedo.

Propping her chin in her clasped hands, she admitted to herself that she hadn't because she was afraid Logan would look as awful as Sanders did in one. Her poor brother looked like Opus the penguin from the cartoon strip in formal dress. But she knew Logan would look just right. Hadn't he just sat there in an Oxford-cloth shirt, buttoned all the way to the neck, and looked just fine? The only other men she'd seen carry that off without looking like they'd lost their nerd packs were Cary Grant and Sam Elliott.

"It fits, I think."

Logan's husky voice made her head snap up. For a moment, she couldn't speak. He looked wonderful in the dark clothing. His golden-brown hair was highlighted by the contrast and now his eyes were more blue than gray. The unconstructed jacket accentuated the width of his shoulders, and she didn't want to even consider what the pants, undoubtedly a size too small, did for the man's thighs. Who cared if David Copperfield had dark hair and gorgeous black eyes after this?

"Yes, it should do nicely," Tory agreed, and got slowly to her feet. Now that the initial shock was over, she noticed that there would have to be some adjustments. He'd buttoned the shirt all the way to the top and the shirt cuffs down. He was also standing ramrod straight, as if he'd been called to attention for inspection. "Just a few changes and you'll be set."

"Who am I?" he asked quietly as she walked around him.

"What?" she said absently, not really hearing his question. She'd suddenly realized what she was going to have to do. She, Victoria Camille Planchet, was going to unbutton the man's shirt halfway to reveal the chest that haunted her dreams, and she would have to touch him to accomplish it. *I really should have gotten the tuxedo.*

"Who am I supposed to be?"

Tory stopped a few inches from him, staring down at his wrists and pretending they weren't centimeters from his well developed thighs. She looked up at him and blinked. "Oh, you're David Copperfield. Haven't you seen him on television?"

"Did he make the Statue of Liberty disappear?"

"That's the one. Give me your hands," Tory ordered while she gave exaggerated attention to the line of his jacket across his shoulders.

He obeyed immediately, holding them out like a child having his hands checked before dinner. Tory stared at the long, sensitive fingers and the light dusting of golden hairs near his wrists, wondering if she could do this with her eyes closed. Taking a deep breath, she reached for his cuff and unbuttoned it without making too much contact with his warm skin beneath. The second one was easier. Then she swallowed heavily and grasped each hand as she pushed the material of his silk shirt and jacket halfway up his arms.

She took a step back, going through the motions of judiciously studying the effect, all the while mustering her courage to touch him again. Thankfully, he was standing as still as a mannequin. "Okay, now we need to loosen a few buttons."

She almost gave a yelp of joy when Logan said, "I'll do it."

"Hmmm, pull out the collar just a little, and we'll see if that does the trick, so to speak," she quipped and gave him an approving grin. He was being so cooperative that she was beginning to wonder why she'd been nervous about the costume.

Logan didn't dare answer her, knowing his voice would come out roughened by his suppressed emotions. He wasn't sure how much longer he could stand having her undivided attention on his body without doing something about it. He let out his breath in relief when she walked behind him, momentarily taking temptation out of sight.

"Hey!" He whirled around as the touch of a slender finger drew a white-hot line down his spine. His affronted exclamation was met by a delicious giggle.

"Sorry I startled you, but you're so stiff. Do all Yankees look like they have a poker stuck, um, to their backbones?" Tory asked with widened brown eyes and an unrepentant grin that raised his blood pressure another twenty points.

"I have excellent posture. It's something to be proud of in Boston," he replied, adjusting his jacket with a show of dignity that also kept his hands busy when all he wanted to do was grab her and shake her. Or kiss her. Anything that would have her in his arms.

"Oh, Logan, it isn't your posture. It's your attitude, I think," she said gently, as if trying not to hurt his feelings.

"What about my attitude? Would it be better if I

slouched, wore suspenders, and scratched my stomach?'' As amazing as it seemed, he realized that she hadn't a clue that she was responsible for his *attitude*.

"You're not posing for a portrait every second of the day. You can relax and still stand up straight," she explained patiently, using her nephew tone again. "Take off the jacket and turn around."

He started to shrug out of the jacket, hoping they would get this torture over with quickly. Then, with the garment halfway down his arms, he gave her a suspicious look over his shoulder. "What are you going to do?"

"Don't worry, this won't hurt."

That's what you think, lady, he mentally shot back, but he tossed aside the jacket anyway. Tory placed her hands tentatively at the back of his neck and began to knead the stiff muscles. Fatalistically, Logan gave himself up to Tory's delightful torture, slowly relaxing under her ministrations.

As she worked her way down his back, he knew he was going to die a slow and painful death. The pants of his outfit had been simply snug when he first put them on. They'd become increasingly uncomfortable with Tory's slim fingers moving freely over his body. He wasn't going to be able to stand much more and maintain the slender hold on his sanity. Another minute and he'd have Tory beneath him on the oversized cabbage roses in the carpet.

"Don't move."

He gladly obeyed. He couldn't have moved if he wanted to without pulling her into his arms, throwing all his noble intentions out the window.

"Now, shake out your arms a little. Very good, Logan. Okay, walk toward me."

Walk? Can I do that? Yes, yes, I can, he discovered, carefully putting one foot in front of the other. It wasn't so difficult, if he focused on the fat cherub on the piano just to the right of Tory's shoulder.

"No, it just won't do. Logan, you walk like you're on a bed of nails," she said, shaking her head and walking toward him clicking her tongue.

Oh, please God, say she isn't. She is. She's going to massage my legs. All rational thoughts left him. What happened was going to happen, he decided, looking down at the top of Tory's head as she knelt at his feet. He might as well enjoy what she was doing. If she did the same thorough job that she'd done on his back, Tory Planchet would be as knowledgeable as his tailor in a matter of minutes. He closed his eyes, knowing a smile was stretching his mouth from ear to ear. *Please, sweetheart, don't stop now.*

Victoria, you're amazing. This is working like a charm, she congratulated herself with complacent satisfaction, her hands working deftly over the taut muscles of Logan's calf. He was being so cooperative, if a little stiff, and doing nothing to follow-up on his visit to her cottage. *Probably thought better of it this morning*, she mused, and concentrated on her task. *Here's one unstuffed Yankee to order, and it's as easy as kneading bread dough.*

She shifted on her knees and moved her hands higher, frowning when Logan tightened up the second she touched his knee. Maybe he's ticklish there, she decided, and continued to work on the problem area until he suddenly groaned. Immediately, she stopped pressing her fingers against the sensitive spot, wondering if she'd hurt him as she tipped back her head to look up. It was a very long way up Logan's lean body.

"I'm sorry, did that hur—" Tory didn't have to finish the question. The fatuous grin on the man's face told her that she hadn't hurt him. Mortification at her naïveté froze her in place, although she could feel her entire body flushing a brilliant red that probably perfectly matched the decor of the sitting room. Her mind was working too well, while her body was at a dead stop.

She'd never been so embarrassed in her entire life, or felt so stupid. Her brain was screaming, *Get up, you silly twit*, and her fingers were attached to the man's thigh as if they'd been smeared with epoxy. If she moved her head ever so slightly to the— No, she wasn't going to even think it.

"Did you want to try the other leg?"

Logan's husky question thankfully brought life back to Tory's legs. In a split second, she backed up without caring that she undoubtedly looked like a crab as she shuffled backward on her knees. Logan's smile and the lazy, sensual message in his hazy-blue gaze made her wonder if she'd ever be able to speak again. She'd just spent the last few minutes feeling up a man without even realizing it; a man who had propositioned her last night after only knowing her for twelve hours. He'd never believe that she hadn't been aware of what she was doing. She was thirty years old and had been kneeling at his feet like a slave girl offering her services.

She refused to look at him, getting up and walking over to the open box that Logan had placed on the ottoman. She fiddled unnecessarily with the tissue paper liner until her restless fingers came into contact with the magic book she'd picked up at the library.

"There's something else you need to do before the party tonight," she said quietly, still not looking at him. He was exactly where she'd left him, staring a hole in her back, judging from the discomfort between her shoulder blades. "You'll have to perform a magic trick before you can eat dessert tonight, or take the consequences. Find a trick in this book and practice it. We'll leave at six-thirty."

"Tory, we're going to talk about this." His smoky voice came from directly beside her, his hand snaking out to pull the book out of her hand. He dropped it onto the ottoman and snared her wrist with his other hand, neatly turning her into his arms. "Nothing's changed since last night, except that I want you more now than ever."

The last words were whispered against her lips. Tory had a glimpse of his hazy-blue eyes igniting into diamond fire before lowering her lashes. It was her last coherent thought. While Logan had been gentle the night before, today he was staking a claim. His lips and tongue branding her, swamping her mind as his arms pulled her snugly into his lean, taut body.

There wasn't any doubt that he desired her as one hand curved around her buttocks, luring her into the cradle of his thighs with a kneading motion. A smoldering ache began low in her body in response to his growing desire. She moved against him instinctively, not sure in her mind if it was to escape or to satisfy her own yearning. Tory knew she shouldn't be in his arms, but her hands didn't agree, moving to circle his neck.

Settling at the nape of his neck, her fingers repeated the same massage that they had long minutes before. At Logan's groan of appreciation, she pressed closer, but the movement only intensified her need. Her body was assailed by thousands of unfamiliar sensations, her blood hot, but sending shivers of desire from head to toe. She knew she'd passed the danger point as her tongue tangled with Logan's in a passionate duet.

Unable to withstand the devastation of his kiss any longer, she tore her mouth away from his. Her breath came in shallow gasps, making it impossible to speak as she gazed up into the angular face of the man who had turned her world upside down in less than twenty-four hours. When he made a slight movement, she pressed her hands against his shoulders to keep him from kissing her again.

"Please, don't say a word," she managed in a hoarse whisper. "This can't be real, Logan. I won't let it be real."

He began to speak, but she forestalled him, placing her fingers on his lips. The gesture was almost her undoing, feeling the warm, moist skin against the pads of her unsteady fingers. "This has to stop. I refuse to become involved with another man like you."

She stepped out of his arms, which loosened at her accusing words. Without a word, she turned and left the room. Tears stung her eyes as she walked out the back door. She knew they were a combination of her emotional reaction to Logan and anger at herself. He'd spelled trouble from the moment he'd stepped into her life, and she wasn't about to let him see her cry.

He wouldn't know that she rarely cried, except when frustrated or extremely angry. Right now, both emotions warred inside her. She was angry at her own stupidity in allowing him to kiss her again. The frustration came from her fear that it would happen again if she spent any time with the damned desirable, exciting man.

"Victoria, you have more sense than that," she stated firmly as she reached the stone walkway to her cottage. "This is one opinionated, arrogant man. You made that mistake once in your life. Logan Herrington is just another Reed Callahan."

The sound of her former fiancé's name on her lips checked her tears. She wasn't going to get involved with another man who would undoubtedly try to rule her life. She had enough of that from blood relatives without welcoming Logan Herrington with open arms. She needed a sensitive, quiet man who would let her live her own life.

From now on, there wouldn't be any physical contact with the man. She was simply her father's stand-in, and if possible, she would introduce Logan to every available woman at the Bush's party, just to insure her safety. He was probably looking for a diversion to relieve his boredom while he was here, and she wasn't going to be his amusement.

The sound of a car horn broke into her dark thoughts just as her hand closed on the latch to the front door. Looking over her shoulder, she swore under her breath. Arnette was back from the grocery store, and the truck was blocking the steps. Logan had clouded her mind so much, she'd forgotten to move the vehicle.

"Where's a good chaperone when you need one," she grumbled, turning to retrace her steps. She had to go back for the truck and help unload the groceries. Before she took two steps, Logan came out the back door and down the steps. Tory knew that he saw her immediately. She shivered in reaction as if his sensitive fingers were moving over her body again. That made up her mind. She turned back to the cottage, leaving Logan to assist Arnette. Later, when the coast was clear, she'd retrieve her costume box from the truck.

FOUR

"So, is it your first lover's quarrel, darlin'? You can tell ole Trevor, can't ya?"

Tory gave her brother a withering look that should have singed the big, floppy ears on his head. The Bush's party was in full swing. Everyone was showing each other magic tricks, whether they knew what they were doing or not. Trust Trevor to notice that his sister and her guest were conspicuous by their lack of participation, and on opposite sides of the huge game room, Tory thought. Right now, he looked harmless enough as he made a glutton of himself on a huge piece of her chocolate cheesecake, but it wouldn't last. She was tempted to smear it all over the white vest and pants of his magician's rabbit costume.

"Buzz off, Eugene," she muttered, quickly regressing to their childhood, and retaliating to his teasing by using his hated middle name. Involuntarily, her gaze strayed across the room to where Logan stood. Like her, he remained a little apart from the mayhem around him.

"Ah, so there *is* trouble in Eden?" Trevor returned,

69

unconcerned by her show of temper. "Come on, tell big brother all your problems. I know some truckers who'd be happy to break one or two of his legs in defense of my sister's honor."

Tory groaned and took her eyes away from the commanding figure across the room. She turned to meet her brother's gaze. His expression was concerned, in spite of his bantering tone. She gave him a slight smile to reassure him that nothing was wrong. "Fool."

"Yeah, well, I was just checking since he has such strange hours for dropping by." Trevor looked almost embarrassed that she'd caught him out, although he'd stood by her before during some emotional upheavals, including her breakup with Reed. "We can't have no stranger comin' into town, messin' with our women folk and gettin' away with it, now can we?"

His poor impersonation of T.L. doing Gary Cooper brought a genuine smile to Tory's lips, and she felt a twinge of guilt that he was trying so hard to cheer her up, even if he had an ulterior motive. Her ill humor was as much her own fault as anything Logan Herrington had done, probably more. She was an independent woman with a mind of her own. A woman who shouldn't allow a kiss to turn her backbone to the consistency of overcooked grits.

She and Logan barely exchanged more than a half dozen words on the way to the party. While she pretended to keep her attention on her driving, Logan had been caught up in his own thoughts. The ten-minute drive had been as tense as their drive from the airport.

"Spare me the macho male routine, Trev, and quit raiding Daddy's B-western tape collection. It's affecting your brain," Tory said, giving him an exaggerated look of disdain. "Humble just doesn't look right on the Planchet bone structure."

"Okay, but don't think I'm going to let this drop. I

expect the full story on our visitor from the North, sooner or later.'' All his usual humor was gone from the assessing look he gave her.

"Down, boy. You're making more out of this than necessary." Tory laughed at his almost villanous look, as if he really would have someone break a few of Logan's bones. "I'm an adult, remember? I know how to handle an arrogant male and a Yankee who just happens to come all in one package."

"That's pretty close to throwing a lit match in a box of dynamite," Trevor agreed. He relaxed again, his wide smile flashing back into place. Almost on reflex, he reached up to rub the bridge of his nose over the spot it had first been broken by his little sister. "Maybe I should warn Logan about what can happen instead. I was only ten years old when you took me on, and I think ole Reed is still trying to get beer out of his ears from the night you ended your engagement."

"I never could take orders very well, but your nose was an accident, even though you'll never let me forget it," she returned indignantly. Trevor just grinned at her. "Now, Reed got what he deserved. Besides, the pitcher of beer was only half full. He just needed to learn that women don't take kindly to being treated like peasants, unless he can find some bimbo that believes his barefoot-and-pregnant philosophy."

"Yes, ma'am. Anything you say, ma'am."

"Turkey. You'd better save that for the next time Arnette finds fault, which will probably be the minute you set foot in the house, or when you find some woman who's crazy enough to take you seriously." She gave him a nasty smile, anticipating her brother's eventual downfall. Then she looked across the room, her gaze immediately meeting Logan's steady regard. She didn't know how long he'd been watching her, but her entire body was suddenly suffused with a warmth that set off tiny sparks along her spine.

Ruthlessly, she ignored those traitorous feelings. She'd behaved like a coward long enough. He was arrogant and overbearing and demanding. But that didn't excuse her behavior, or the fact she'd taken the easy way out by ignoring him, leaving him to his own devices at the party. She'd been taught to be gracious even in the most difficult circumstances. Abandoning Logan in a room full of strangers wasn't something she was proud of doing. It certainly didn't prove anything about her will power either, if she resisted him simply by avoiding him.

"Well, big brother, while you feed your face, I have to go rescue our guest from annihilation by an angry husband."

"Can I sell tickets?" Trevor asked with a eager grin. "This could be a major event."

"I know a few truckers myself, Trev, old boy. Remember Dwayne and Little Otis?" Tory returned, giving him a challenging look by raising a single eyebrow. "For that crack, you're going to go pry Button Mainwairing off Logan's chest."

"Uh-oh, she's on the prowl again," he murmured as he followed the direction of Tory's unconscious glare. The twice-divorced, raven-haired woman had just slithered up to Logan. "You'll owe me big for this one, Tory. Although I guess I don't have to worry about you that much since Curtiss and Logan are going to Oklahoma in about thirty-six hours."

"Oklahoma?" Tory couldn't keep the surprise out of her voice.

"The Cherokee Challenge at Grove, remember? Curtiss is going to give Logan a preview of rally racing before the Arkansas Traveler," Trevor explained, emphasizing each word as a taunting smile spread over his lips again. "Maybe I should start taking advice from this guy, instead of planning to beat him to a pulp. He's only been here two days, and he's already got you—"

"Trevor Eugene Planchet," Tory began in a dangerous growl, dragging her eyes away from Logan's pleading look for rescue as Button ran scarlet tipped fingers over his chest.

"All right, all right," her brother begged in surrender and threw up his hands. "I'll go draw off the two-bit vamp, but I'll leave you with this advice. You might want to lower the zipper on your jumpsuit a little, and you definitely want to wipe off the remaining half of your Henning mustache if you want Logan to stay interested."

He quickly made his way toward Logan before she had a chance to object. But she had more than Trevor's teasing on her mind. She had to be cool and composed when she faced Logan. Fleetingly she wondered if keeping T.L. out of her business affairs was really worth it. Logan Herrington was much more than she bargained for when she drove to the airport yesterday, and he was here for three months.

"Now admit it, Logan, you did have a good time," Tory announced, smiling pleasantly up at her companion as they walked away from the Bush's front door to her station wagon. She was feeling very pleased with herself, and the world at large after a few relaxing hours with her friends. She'd regained her equilibrium by treating Logan as if he were one of her brothers. They'd managed to have an enjoyable evening after the rocky start. Logan turned out to be an amusing escort.

"Come on, didn't you enjoy yourself just a teeny, tiny, little bit? Whoops."

Logan smothered a laugh, grasping her firmly under the elbow as she stumbled on the uneven surface of the driveway. "Just how may wine spritzers did you have?"

Tory looked back over her shoulder at the offending gravel that had rolled under her sneaker while she thought over his question. She turned back to him, straightening her posture with exaggerated care, but couldn't dislodge his hand. "I had three—two white and one rosé. A southern lady doesn't over indulge in any activity or substance."

"I thought we agreed to drop the North/South rivalry after Gary Bush named me an honorary southerner," he commented, still trying to suppress his amusement, and retaining a firm hold on her elbow. "It was the least he could do after I won the prize for the best magic trick."

"So he did, against my better judgment. Still, I'm sure it holds true for any lady, in any place. Now, where did I put the car keys?" She patted her hands down the length of her turquoise jumpsuit under Logan's interested gaze. The movement allowed her to step away from him, giving her a respite from the tingling sensation in her arm. "Ah, here they are. This jumpsuit has too many pockets."

"Wouldn't it be a good idea for me to drive? Gary made me pledge to be protective of the ladies."

"Gary got a little carried away because he's only been married a year. He and Abby don't know the honeymoon is over and are attached at the hip," Tory stated with a grimace, but she handed him the keys without an argument. "I assure you that I'm perfectly capable of driving. My basic problem with alcohol is it makes me relax or get very honest, sometimes both. I think you just want to drive the 'Woody.' I saw your covetous look earlier."

"You've found me out. A friend of mine at Princeton had a beauty like this. About a 1946 model, isn't it?" Logan waited for her nod, then continued his confession. "Unfortunately, Nathan wouldn't let anyone touch it, not even when he washed it." He opened the passenger door with a flourish, and Tory slid bonelessly into the car.

On impulse, she captured his hand where it rested on the open window frame. "Ya know, Logan, I think I might like you after all, no matter why you're here."

She regretted the words the minute they were out of her mouth. Logan's easy smile vanished. His whole body stiffened as the lines deepened in his angular face. There was almost a stricken look in his eyes, but Tory dismissed the thought, blaming it on the poor light from the yard lamp. It was simply his usual neutral expression. Suddenly she was angry with Preston Herrington. The man might be very ill, but how could he do this to his nephew? She didn't know why Logan was here, but the reason had hurt him badly, although she was sure he wouldn't admit it even to himself.

Shaken more than she cared to consider, Tory came to a decision. She was going to help Logan with whatever the problem was. Her voice came out low and intent. "Logan Herrington, don't you dare turn into some grim-faced Puritan on me."

He stopped trying to pull away from her grasp. Tory loosened her hold slightly, sure that he wouldn't move away. He was staring down at her in open mouthed amazement. Fleetingly, she wondered if anyone had ever seen him in such an unsophisticated pose. He worked his mouth for a minute, as if experimenting to see if it still worked. Before he could utter a sound, a group of partiers came out of the Bush's front door.

"I refuse to be caught arguing in the driveway. The Herringtons have more dignity than that," he muttered, pulling his hand out from Tory's relaxed grip. He turned abruptly on his heels and stalked around the station wagon, gravel scattering under his rapid strides.

Tory waved to her friends, answering their farewells as Logan gunned the engine. She wasn't sure what to do next. Slumping down in her seat, she fiddled with the seatbelt buckle and wondered if she dared to open her mouth again. The soft night breeze from the open window cooled her flushed cheeks as she considered her alternatives. Always one to charge her way through a situation, she decided to press on.

"Did you really learn that trick with the pitcher of milk and the newspaper this afternoon, or did you cheat, and know magic before tonight?" She kept her tone light, hoping he wouldn't know how much she resisted the urge to blurt out, *Why did Preston send you to Arkansas?* Besides, they couldn't keep having these stony silences every time they got into a car together.

"A magician doesn't tell his secrets, young woman. It wouldn't be magic anymore if everyone knew how the tricks were done," Logan finally answered, just when she was about to give up hope. "Some of us take professional pride in our work."

"Is that comment directed at me?" Tory asked eagerly. She sat up and turned to face him, hooking her left leg up on the seat.

"If the trick fits. Aggie magic? You call yourself a magician by holding up two fingers on each hand, putting them behind your back, and then holding up one finger on one hand and three on the other?" Logan made a clicking noise of disgust with his tongue, shaking his head at Tory's idea of a magic trick.

"Hey, I got laughter and applause, didn't I? What more could a performer want?" She grinned without a show of remorse, beginning to relax again because he was smiling, adapting to their nonsensical talk without batting an eyelash. There was humor in the man, and he could enjoy the ridiculous. Would she still be this pleased about this tomorrow with a clear head?

"Besides, how can you criticize my act when you don't even know what an Aggie is?" she argued, testing to see how long they could continue discussing a subject of absolutely no importance or redeeming quality. Tomorrow was soon enough to worry about the consequences.

"Do so," Logan shot back, flashing a knowing grin in her direction.

"Do not," she returned, her mind not fully on the matter at hand. He'd just shown her that he possessed more than just one lethal weapon to disturb her sleep. Not only did he have a chest that should be outlawed and give kisses that paralyzed all rational thought, he had a playful grin that was downright outrageous.

"An Aggie is a person of undetermined intellect who attends Texas A & M University. Such persons are treated with little, or no respect, and thought by most Arkansans, er, Arkansianians, whatever, to be subhuman."

"Somebody told you, didn't they?" Tory placed her arm along the back of the seat and laid her head in the crook of her arm. She was enjoying herself immensely, no matter how dangerous that was, but she was beginning to feel sleepy just as she had predicted.

"Again, as a reporter, I can't reveal my sources," Logan returned smoothly, eliciting a sleepy groan of frustration from the lady.

She's gone to sleep, Logan thought as he glanced at Tory's heart-shaped face relaxed in slumber. A feeling of warmth rushed over him, laying to rest the frustration he'd been feeling all night watching Tory smile and joke with her friends. Somehow in less than forty-eight hours this nicely curved brunette with maple-syrup eyes had him all tied up in knots. One minute she smiled at him mischievously, the next she'd stare at him coldly, and then suddenly seem contrite.

Victoria Camille Planchet was beyond his comprehension. The past two days were almost a fantasy, out of his range of experience. Preston had really outdone himself this time by playing the omnipotent deity. The older man's words still echoed in his brain: *At least act like a human being with blood running through your veins instead of a preppy android.* Well, the old buzzard should be laughing himself silly by now. In only two days, Logan had experienced anger, frustration, and absolute confusion. Those all qualified as honest-to-god emotions—along with passion, want, and need. All these emotions were running rampant.

With another glance at Tory's sleeping figure, he wasn't sure he wanted it any other way. When she and Trevor rescued him from the cloying woman with the unlikely name of Button, he determined that he'd try to go easy again. He grimaced at himself in the rearview mirror, remembering how quickly Tory had made him forget his good intentions that afternoon. He wasn't going to do it this time. He knew how to conduct a civilized relationship with a woman and had never before found it necessary to grab a woman into his arms. It just wasn't dignified.

He was a Herrington. The Herringtons were *the* example of how to behave. His mother had drilled into his head that he should always remember his name and fine ancestry even under the most adverse conditions. Herringtons were leaders, role models for those less fortunate—those who weren't Herringtons. The only problem was that Enid Herrington had never told him how a Herrington should react to physical desire. He pictured his slender, elegantly pale, blond-haired mother, and wondered if she'd felt desire for any man in the twenty years since his father had died, or even before that.

"You're on your own for this one, old boy," he muttered and stopped the car at the closed gate of the Planchet property.

"Logan?" Tory's question was soft and drowsy. He knew it was a sound he wanted to hear again when they woke up together following an unforgettable night in each other's arms.

"The gate's closed." His voice was huskier than usual.

"Oh, the code is two, three, four, eleven."

In a matter of minutes they arrived at the main house. Logan turned off the engine, but didn't make a move to leave the car. He turned to his companion, who'd snuggled back to sleep. Gently he feathered a finger over the fringe of her bangs and down her cheek, pushing her hair back from her soft cheek to loop behind her ear. She smiled as though his touch pleased her. Unfortunately, he knew he couldn't sit here all night staring at Tory in the moonlight, even though she seemed content to stay right where she was.

"Tory?" His soft question had no effect. He tried again in a conversational tone, brushing her cheek with the side of his finger.

"Inna minute," she mumbled, batting away his hand with a wide sweep of her hand.

"We can't stay here all night." Logan gave a resigned sigh, knowing what he was going to have to do. He restarted the car and drove the short distance to the cottage. Tory didn't stir once, even when he repeated her name three times. She simply burrowed deeper into the seat.

Logan climbed out of the car, wondering how much one man could possibly endure. "How can anyone find the front seat of a car comfortable?"

When he reached the other side of the car, he stopped for a minute to asses the situation. He wasn't going to carry Tory over a pitch dark stone walkway to end up at a locked door. Giving the sleeping figure another look, he turned and headed for the cottage. The key box was above the lintel, the second place he looked. Entering the house, he turned on lights as he searched for Tory's bedroom.

Standing on the threshold of the room, he knew he should immediately turn around and go shake Tory awake. It was a room that he'd like in his own townhouse; a room where he wanted to make love to Tory. A mahogany field bed, draped with a crocheted canopy, dominated the room. He forced himself to look around the rest of the cream-and-rose colored room. By admiring the Empire dressing bureau and enclosed basin stand, he wouldn't think about the soft bundle of femininity who lived here, and who he'd soon carry through the doorway. Absently he remembered Tory's comment about smuggling most of the Hepplewhite and Duncan Phyfe pieces from the main house.

Walking slowly back to the car, he wondered—not for the first time—about the Planchet family. It kept his mind off how inviting the canopied bed looked, even without Tory in it. Most of the furniture in the main house and cottage weren't reproductions, but authentic antiques. Where had they come from, and what did T.L. do for a living?

Furniture and T.L.'s occupation were forgotten as soon as he opened the passenger door. At a light touch on her shoulder, Tory turned trustingly into his arms, wrapping her arms around his neck. Logan kept his body rigid as he carried her up the walkway, wondering what he'd done to deserve such exquisite torture. Tory snuggled her head into the crook of his shoulder, her breath warm on his neck.

With long strides, he made it into the bedroom in record time. In a Herculean effort, he kept from dropping Tory when she nuzzled the sensitive skin under his ear, murmuring, "So nice."

What, or who, was nice he didn't care as he laid her on the bed. He watched in fascination as she wiggled to find a comfortable spot on the flowered comforter. When she frowned and shifted to another position, Logan knew he was doomed. Tory reached up to pull at the material of her jumpsuit.

"Being a gentleman doesn't pay, Herrington. You should have hightailed it out of here the minute you put her down," he told himself, rubbing the back of his neck and glaring at the cause of his problem. The jumpsuit that fit Tory like a second skin had silver spangles on it; spangles that were rubbing against her soft skin.

"You're an absolute fool." Reluctantly he bent over to begin the arduous task of undressing Tory. The way his luck was running she'd wake up during his mission of mercy and assume the worst. Luck, and possibly the influence of the wine spritzers, were on his side with the added help of the garment's network of zippers. He made short work of stripping off the jumpsuit, trying not to notice the alluring figure beneath, or the scraps of satin and lace that were her only covering.

Before he could consider the alternative, Logan walked to the other side of the bed and quickly flipped the comforter over Tory. It was much safer than reaching across her and giving into the temptation to join her. With the comforter partially covering her glorious skin and bits of lingerie, he moved back around the bed to complete his task.

As a reward for his good behavior, he lingered for one last look. Tory was as desirable in sleep as she was awake. His new knowledge of the exact shape of her lovely breasts and the perfection of her hips and legs didn't help matters. Stifling a groan and cursing his noble upbringing, he ducked his head under the fringed canopy to give Tory a chaste goodnight kiss.

He snapped off the lights on his hasty retreat from the cottage, making sure the front door was locked before he headed for the car. As he started the engine, he decided that apricot lace would haunt him for the rest of the night, if not his entire life.

*   *   *

The shrill ringing of the bedside phone roused Tory from an exquisite dream. Unfortunately, the phone was insistent, shattering the last remnants of sleep and the vision of a mysterious stranger carrying her in his arms. Without opening her eyes, she reached for the offending instrument on the Pembroke table.

" 'Lo'," was all she managed before subsiding back into the pillows.

"Tory? Is that you?" Leeanne asked anxiously after a brief hesitation.

"Mmmmmm."

"You're still in bed at eleven-thirty? Are you sick?"

"Eleven-thirty? It can't be," Tory exclaimed and shot up to a sitting position, opening her eyes only to shut them against the bright light of the room. Why were the shades open? Cautiously she opened her eyes again, looking around the room as her vision adjusted to the light. The shades weren't the only thing wrong. She couldn't understand why she was wearing her bra and panties and sleeping on top of the bed covers.

"Tory, are you still there?"

"Yes, Leeanne, I was just trying to clear my head. You sound upset. Is something wrong?"

"Not really. Curtiss asked me to call you because he has an emergency on his hands," the other woman said in a rush. "He needs you to do him a favor. Oh, Ty Daniel, how could you? Hang on a minute, Tory."

Tory didn't have much choice since her sister-in-law put down the phone without waiting for a response. While she waited for her nephew's latest crime to be handled, she tried to unravel the mystery of her sleeping apparel. She couldn't remember going to bed and it puzzled her. Last night had been the Bush's party. Logan drove them home and—

"Sorry about that, but Ty Daniel decided to cut his

hair," Leeanne said breathlessly into the phone. "I managed to catch him before he actually did any damage. Now, where were we?"

"Curtiss wants me to do him a favor," Tory prompted, *and I was trying to figure out how I got to bed last night and what Logan had to do with it*.

"Curtiss needs you to take Logan to Oklahoma tomorrow. He's got a problem with one of the Atlinger's quarter horses," the other woman explained, then waited for a response. "Tory, is there a problem with that?"

"What? Oh, Curtiss wants me to do what?" Tory practically shouted the question into the phone as the meaning of Leeanne's words sank in at exactly the same moment that she realized what had happened the night before. Logan Herrington undressed her, down to her sheerest underwear, and put her to bed.

"He wants you to take Logan to the Oklahoma rally for him. The horse might have colic, and he's Atlinger's prize stud. They'll lose a fortune if Morning Star dies. Curtiss has to stay here until the crisis passes," Leeanne answered.

"Good Lord, is he crazy?"

"Please, Tory, you know he wouldn't ask if it wasn't absolutely necessary, and you're the only one with the free time to do it."

"All right, all right. I'll call you back later for the details. Bye," Tory said quickly, and hung up before Leeanne could lengthen the conversation. She had a lot to think about, and it all concerned Mr. Logan Herrington.

A brief glance at the undented pillow next to her gave her the small assurance that she'd slept alone. Tossing back the comforter she headed for the shower, hoping it would clear her head even more and bring back total recall of the previous night.

The quick shower and fresh clothing didn't make any difference. Tory couldn't remember a thing beyond a silly conversation in the car about magic tricks. Still tying the belt to her moss-green cotton romper, she headed for the main house in search of some answers.

"I knew I was going to regret being nice to him last night," she grumbled, stomping across the lawn. "Who would've thought a properly bred Bostonian would turn out to be a voyeur? Yankee manners!"

She trotted up the back steps and through the back door, her temper escalating with each stride. When she spotted Arnette arranging flowers in the front hall, she demanded, "Where is he?"

"Oh, good morning, dear, or should I say good afternoon," the older woman said, not bothering to look up from the carnations she was separating. "You just missed Mrs. Carter's call. She wants to go with the all seafood menu after all, and she wants the salmon mousse with dill sauce as well."

"Where is he?" Tory repeated and dismissed her best client's wishes—a prominent member of the Opera Guild—as if she were a pesky gnat.

"Are you looking for Logan? He's not here."

"Not here? Where did he go?" *That rat's hiding from me.*

"He had an interview with a Mr. Kowalski," Arnette explained as she stepped back to survey her handiwork. "I think he said something about blind hams and an interesting story. Does that make any sense to you?"

"Blind hams? Oh, the radio operators for the rally. One of the ham radio clubs has quite a few members who are blind," Tory returned, but her mind still wasn't on what she was saying. "Damn the man."

"Victoria Camille."

The reprimand brought Tory's attention back to the other woman, who was standing with her hands on her hips, a frown marring her round face. The stance made Tory realize she'd sworn out loud.

"What's gotten into you, young lady? You've been madder than a wet hen since Mr. Herrington arrived. You haven't been this short tempered since you sent that Callahan fella on his way."

"Trust me, Arnette, the two have a lot in common," Tory answered, then decided she'd said too much. "I'll be at the Park Plaza shop for the rest of the day. Tell *Mr. Herrington* that I'll see him at dinner."

She turned on her heels and left the house before Arnette could start asking questions. Her own words were echoing in her brain. Reed and Logan were poles apart in appearance, but they were both opinionated men. That was enough for her. She'd broken her engagement six years ago because she didn't want a man running her life, and she'd been wary of any close relationships since misjudging Reed.

They'd met in college and shared interests. Although they knew they'd be separated for a year after graduation, Reed had proposed a week before commencement. He'd been set to go to his apprenticeship in California and Tory to Paris. The moment he put the ring on her finger, the trouble began. Suddenly, he objected to her trip to France, although he'd seemed enthusiastic about her additional training only the week before. He said he didn't want his woman gallivanting around a foreign country without his protection. Tory went despite his disapproval. After battling T.L. during most of her formative years, she wasn't about to let Reed sway her from her purpose.

The engagement lasted a year, most of which they were separated. Tory liked to think she had more brains than to remain tied to such a chauvinistic jerk. Her first week back from Paris, Reed came to Little Rock and found fault with everything and everyone. After two days, Tory knew she'd made a tremendous mistake. He treated her as if she only had half a brain and was put on the earth to fetch and carry for him. One evening they went out with some of her high school friends, arguing on the way to the restaurant, and returning home in separate cars. Reed was dripping wet from the beer Tory poured on him after one patronizing remark too many. She'd been extremely satisfied with her handy work.

After Reed, she'd evaluated exactly what type of man she wanted in her life. He'd be quiet, sensitive, and understanding. The man she married, if she married, would be supportive and caring. None of these characteristics had anything to do with a self-possessed Yankee who had the nerve to undress a woman when she was unconscious. That was something an amazing chest and bone-melting kisses couldn't make up for, Tory decided.

Tonight she would lay down the ground rules for the rest of Logan's visit once and for all. And if that didn't work, maybe she'd resort to a pitcher of beer again—a full one this time.

FIVE

Logan took his eyes off the straight stretch of highway in front of him to study his traveling companion. Tory was slumped down in her seat with her feet braced against the dashboard and a new baseball cap pulled down over her eyes. She hadn't said more than a dozen saccharin-sweet words to him since she arrived at the house with the Winnebago and handed him the keys. He knew she was angry with him and why, but his mind kept wandering to dangerous territory. Was she wearing another set of mind-boggling lingerie under her jeans and cotton blouse?

Clearing his throat as they passed a mileage sign to Fort Smith, he knew they couldn't go on like this for another four or five hours. He also had to get his mind off the vision of Tory in her bedroom. "If I apologize, will you start talking to me again without smothering me with southern charm?"

She uncrossed her arms and tipped her cap back enough to uncover one eye. "I was just being polite."

"Tory, you're madder than hell about me putting you to bed the other night, and we both know it," Logan said without hesitation. "I'm sure if I'd been around yesterday, or hadn't gone out to dinner with Trevor, we'd have had this out already."

"Okay," she answered, sitting up and readjusting her cap. Turning to face him, she hooked her leg up onto the console. "I was spitting mad yesterday morning when I woke up and realized that an absolute stranger undressed me. Of course, it didn't help that I'd just learned I was going on a three-day trip with the same person."

"I really didn't look, at least no more than necessary. The Herringtons have set the standard for good manners in Boston for over two hundred years." Logan flinched at his own words, he'd gone from lame to pompous in a matter of seconds. "You really shouldn't worry so much, you have a beautiful body." *Oh, Lord, that makes it even worse.*

"I knew I should have taken Trevor up on his offer."

Logan wished he dared look to see Tory's expression, but he had to keep his eye on the car in front of them that was slowing for the exit. "What did he offer to do?"

"He knows some truckers that might be willing to break a few of your bones," she announced quite happily. "You'd only shown up on my doorstep at midnight when he offered."

"I can imagine. He gave me a rather cautionary brotherly talk last night."

"He did?"

"Mmmmm-hmmmm. He explained that young women of the southern persuasion were delicate flowers that had been gently nurtured." Logan schooled his features to be properly earnest, just as Trevor's had been. He knew it was a red herring, but Tory was talking to him. It would also be nice to have her mad at someone else for a change.

"Tell me he didn't, please?" Tory begged in a tone that told Logan he'd succeeded in diverting her.

"He didn't mention any names, if that's any comfort." His lips twitched slightly at Tory's answering groan. "And he had this curious habit of fingering his steak knife during the entire conversation."

"It's definitely time for Dwayne and Little Otis."

"Who?"

"I have some truckers of my own, if necessary," she said with a hint of pride.

"Does this mean you're still mad at me?"

"Just don't let it happen again," she warned, but he could detect some humor in her tone.

Logan didn't realize until that moment how tense he'd been, his body stiff as his hands clenched the steering wheel. He made a conscious effort to relax, but cautioned himself to be on his guard. There was the ever-present danger of putting his foot in his mouth again. "So, how does a delicate flower meet truckers?"

"They're delivery men for the construction crew that's working on my shops." The pride was back in her words tenfold.

"Your shops? What do you sell?"

"Food, wonderful food. I have a catering business that I'm expanding to include three retail stores," she explained easily, and Logan knew that he'd picked the right subject, for once. "In fact, if we have time on the way back I want to stop at Wiederkehrs vineyards to see about handling some of their wines in the shops."

"Who's your clientele?" He decided not to ask about the quality of Arkansas wines since the conversation was going so well.

"Mostly singles, or people who don't like to cook or have the time to do something out of the ordinary. Trevor suggested it after I'd been getting requests for private dinners, as well as the usual parties and receptions." Tory laughed suddenly, catching Logan by surprise. "Actually, Trevor was my inspiration. He kept conning me into making him elegant dinners for two. I'm sure there are some delicately nurtured flowers out there who were led astray by my big brother after a dinner I prepared."

"So, that's why you have so much free time. I was beginning to wonder if you were on vacation."

"Not really. I've slowed down operations while the shops are being renovated, and I'm at the mercy of my family's sob stories. That's why I'm on the way to Oklahoma in a motor home."

"Why are we using this anyway? I admit I'm getting used to finding a different vehicle every time I go somewhere." Logan had forgotten to ask Trevor about the car situation the night before, and about T.L.'s profession. "Trevor showed up yesterday morning in a 1956 Thunderbird. This Winnebago is the first vehicle your family has that isn't over twenty years old."

"It's T.L.'s way of keeping up with the Rockefellers, though he has quite a way to go before he has anything like the museum over on Petit Jean Mountain," Tory answered, seeming to forget her earlier animosity. "The truck and station wagon are his, along with about fifteen other cars of various ages. The T-bird belongs to me and Trevor. We trade off every three months and drive one of T.L.'s in the meantime. As for our current mode of transport, it belongs to Curtiss, and I haven't the faintest idea why he said to take it."

"What exactly does T.L. do for a living?" He was certain that there was more to his uncle's old friend, and perhaps his profession could give him a clue. The Planchets were an influential family and vintage cars weren't cheap.

"Oh, dear, hasn't anyone told you?"

"Is it illegal? Preston didn't tell me anything beyond

my assignment, and Trevor was talking car rallies when he wasn't giving advice.''

"Daddy's in garbage.''

Logan took his eyes off the road to give Tory a skeptical look. She was grinning from ear to ear.

"He really is. His corporation runs one of the largest waste hauling firms in the Southwest,'' she went on, not bothering to hide her amusement at his flabber-gasted expression. "Don't worry, it kind of hits every-one that way if they don't know before they meet him.''

"Apparently they didn't meet him the way I did,'' Logan said dryly, giving her a pained smile. "Or does he only do that for visitors from the North?''

"Yes, well, Daddy has a strange sense of humor at times,'' she stated, matching his tone and shrugging. "Did Trevor or Curtiss give you any instructions about the race tomorrow?''

Logan could tell she wanted to change the subject, and he gladly complied. He did promise himself they would get back to the subject of T.L., although he wasn't anxious to dwell on it right now. It could lead to the reason he was in Arkansas, which he didn't want to discuss yet. He'd finally managed to get on solid, fairly compatible ground with Tory. His exile to the South wasn't something he wanted to talk about until he'd known her a little longer.

Without hesitation, he launched into the explanation Trevor had given him about the similarities and differ-ences between the Cherokee Challenge and the Arkan-sas Traveler. It was a safe subject, and he could question Tory about her part in the rallies for his articles as well.

He still had a lot to learn about this form of racing since he'd only seen the European version on television. How was a standard street car modified to withstand the rough terrain of dirt roads that were specially selected for each stage of the race? How were the cars timed on each stage, and what were the regulations for driving on public roads between stages? Was it true that the driver with the fastest accumulated time wouldn't be named the winner if he'd been penalized for starting too soon, or driving too fast between stages? Were the stages run during the day, then repeated over the same ground at night to test the skill of the driver? That should keep them occupied for a good portion of the trip.

As he conversed easily with Tory for almost the first time since they had met, he wondered when he'd spent this much time talking with an individual. He was sure that Preston would be pleased. In Boston, he never seemed to have time for this type of communication. His conversations were with H.P.G. employees, or brief comments in passing at some function his mother had organized. It seemed as though he'd spent more time interacting with people as individuals in the past four days than he had in years. Underlying his discovery was amused speculation over what his mother's reaction would be when she discovered *those people* were in the garbage business.

Tory surveyed the motel room that was wall-to-wall people; the crowd a mixture of drivers, crew members, and organizers. Tonight they partied and told wild stories, then tomorrow they drove, partying again afterward with more wild stories of the day's events. There were a few familiar faces from the last time she headed a timing crew—and one very familiar face.

Logan was standing near the beer keg talking to Harry Scranton, who was in charge of the radio operators. His face was intent as he listened to the older man. They both were oblivious to the redhead who draped herself provocatively against the door jamb behind them. Tory wasn't.

"Little Miss Tory isn't enjoying herself," announced

a gruff voice in her ear, taking her attention away from the trio on the other side of the room.

"Will I ever be old enough to lose that name, Alf?" she asked the balding man of fifty standing next to her.

"Nope, I can still see the freckled-face, pig-tailed little monster who was eating a candy apple near my leather upholstery." His pained expression showed he clearly remembered the afternoon T.L. had brought his daughter along to inspect Alf's Dussenberg. "And that's why I made sure your friend over there is bunking with Harve Waggoner."

"Does he snore?"

"I don't know, does he?" His blue eyes twinkled with amusement and interest.

"Alf, you old scamp," Tory returned, refusing to be drawn in.

"Would you be happier if Harve did snore? If that smart-looking Yankee is giving you any problems, I can make better arrangements."

"No, Logan's been a perfect gentleman." *Damn him*, she finished to herself. The man had her more confused now than he had the night he showed up on her doorstep. They'd spent hours cooped up in the front of the Winnebago, conversing like old friends. If she'd met Logan today for the first time, she'd have liked him without reservation.

"You don't need to worry about Midge Nesbitt, although I think you've singed her around the edges a little with that ladylike glare," Alf observed. "She's just bored because Walt's wrapped up in the other room watching old racing videos. She's not really on the look out for a new co-driver for the night."

"It's none of my concern," Tory stated with more conviction than she felt. She wanted to go over and tell Midge to get bored someplace else besides sidling up next to Logan, but she didn't want to acknowledge the possessive feelings that were fueling her anger. It was bad enough that she'd let the incident of Logan putting her to bed go by so easily. A scene would have been anticlimactic, or so she told herself, because she hadn't been able to confront him until almost a day later.

"The boy might not know about car rallies, but he does have class. I don't think I've ever seen a man brush off a woman like that, and have her smiling about it," Alf commented in admiration as Logan disengaged himself from Midge and the group he'd been talking with for the past half hour. "I've seen that woman practically take the skin off a control crew that didn't do things her way. She's a demon for getting any time she can shaved off by fair means, or foul."

"She goes with Walt?" Tory asked and gave the curvaceous redhead with perfectly manicured, two-inch fingernails a searching look. It wasn't that much of a surprise, but it kept her from thinking about Logan's tall figure, which was headed straight toward her and Alf.

"Honey, she's ranked in the top five co-drivers nationally," the older man explained, laughing at Tory's grimace. "And be glad you're a spectator tomorrow, instead of working one of the controls, 'cause she's not happy your fella left her. Apparently he didn't manage it as smoothly as I thought from the look she's giving him."

Tory didn't get a chance to look because Logan was beside her, his arm curling unexpectedly around her shoulders.

"Help, please," he murmured in her ear, seeming to whisper a tender greeting to anyone who was watching. "That woman is on the prowl, and her boyfriend outweighs me by about a hundred pounds."

"Alf says she's just bored," Tory informed him, ignoring the delightful shiver under the surface of her skin as his warm breath teased her hair near her ear. "Isn't that right, Alf?"

"Let's just say that she's never messed with me," he returned. His blue eyes were watching the pair in front of him too intently for Tory's comfort. "Besides, Walt's as gentle as a lamb, and I'm old enough to be her daddy."

"We must do things differently in Boston. Just how gentle would he be if he found me helping his lady friend fix a burned-out light over her bed?"

"How fond are you of your nose, an eye, and possibly a few ribs?" Alf's face was somber as he posed the question. "Now keep in mind that Grove doesn't have a hospital, although maybe there's a doctor on the reservation who'd take a look at you. Considering that, you made the right decision, but Tory darlin', you need to get both arms around him, just in case."

"Sounds good to me," Logan agreed, placing his other arm around her, his hand resting lightly above her hip bone.

Tory wanted to take back every kind thought she'd had about Logan. The warmth of his hand was burning through her blouse and the denim of her new jeans. Her first impulse was to tell him to move it or lose it, but Alf was watching them too closely. Instead, she smiled placidly.

"You know, Alf, this is Logan's first rally, and I think that deserves a special treat tomorrow," she began sweetly, leaning her head on Logan's shoulder for good measure before looking up at him with an innocent smile. "How about giving him a place in the first sweep car?"

"The *first* sweep? Oh, I see," he managed over the sudden blare of music as someone turned up the radio. His amused glance met Tory's so he kept the correct phrase "fast sweep" to himself. He was willing to play along if the lady wanted Logan in the pace car that drove over the various stages at close-to-racing speed while making sure the road was clear before starting the rally. "That's no problem at all. I'll check with Tod Blaylock."

"Good. You'll get a really good perspective of the race that way," Tory informed Logan. She hoped tomorrow's course was over roads as dusty and hilly as the dirt-logging roads they used in Arkansas. That would teach him to use her as a decoy.

"Well, ya'll, I think I'm going to turn in. It was a long drive today, and for some reason I always feel worse when I'm a passenger than when I drive," she said, taking the chance to move away from Logan's disturbing touch.

"The driver thinks that's a good idea," Logan agreed, and matched her step for step toward the door.

"Here, Logan, you'll need the key."

Tory barely managed to suppress a giggle at Logan's puzzled expression. He looked at the key in Alf's hand as if it were a repellant insect.

"Alf managed to get you a bed in Harve Waggoner's room, and he can guarantee that he doesn't snore," she explained with a wide-eyed look. "It's so nice to have one of T.L.'s old friends around, isn't it?"

"Certainly," Logan managed, his narrowed gaze moving from Tory to a beaming Alf. "I'll walk you to the Winnebago and get my bag."

The hooded look he gave her made Tory lose some of her amusement. "It could have been worse, you know. You might have had to bunk down in here with about ten or so people."

"How true. We'll see you both at breakfast, then," Alf put in and handed Logan his key.

Tory decided discretion was the better part of valor, and didn't say a word as they walked out the door.

They were parked about four rooms down from the rally headquarters. Logan kept a courteous hand at Tory's back during the short walk, letting the silence between them continue. Tory tried to pretend the hand at the small of her back didn't make her blood sing, or bring back memories of the two times she'd been in his arms.

Although they'd just left a roomful of people behind, she suddenly felt isolated from the entire world in the quiet, moonlit parking lot. The Cozy Grove Motel was along the main road, but they might well have been in a ghost town. If she dared, she'd have done an about-face and returned to the party. There was safety in numbers.

When they reached the motor home, Logan took the keys from her and opened the door. He waved her up the steps without a word. Once inside, he quickly found the canvas tote bag he'd brought and stored behind the driver's seat. Tory stood in the middle of the carpeted living area, not sure what to do next. Crossing her arms over her breasts, she braced herself for whatever was going to happen next.

"Well, I'm all set. Do you need any help making up your bed?" Logan turned to her, his eyebrows raised in mild inquiry.

"Ah, no. I just have to pull out the couch that's along the back." Even in the bright overhead light she couldn't detect any hidden meaning in his words and his face was that of a man who didn't have a care in the world.

"Fine. I'll see you in the morning then."

He was gone before Tory realized it. The outside door shut with a mocking click. She dropped her arms and stared in amazement, feeling like an absolute fool. He had to know she was expecting him to kiss her, or at least try, and she'd been planning on how to avoid it. In one furious stride, she reached the door and snapped the lock. Then she marched over to the couch in two steps, throwing herself down on the striped cushion.

"What's he up to now?" she asked the empty room, drawing her knees up to her chin. *And why am I so upset that he didn't even try to touch me*?

Knowing she wasn't going to like the answer, she jumped to her feet again. If she kept busy, she wouldn't have to think about *him*. Unfortunately, her temper helped her secure the Winnebago for sleeping in record time. The bed was open and the screen placed behind the driver's seat in a matter of minutes. Ten minutes later she had her face washed, teeth brushed, and was pulling on her nightshirt.

She stared at the bed with a jaundiced eye, knowing that she wasn't ready to go to sleep. The only reading material available was two coloring books that belonged to Ty Daniel and Amanda Sue. Why didn't she pack a book this morning? She knew the answer, the same answer to everything else in her life for the last four days—Logan Winchester Herrington, VI. She'd been working up her nerve to see him again while she packed and barely remembered the necessities.

There wasn't anything else to do but go to bed. She lay in the dark listening to the crickets and an occasional car passing on the road in front of the motel. Now he was going to give her insomnia because she knew if she closed her eyes, Logan would play a prominent part in her dreams.

"Damn him," she muttered, punching at her pillow, then turning on her side. Closing her eyes, she was determined she wasn't going to let the man ruin her sleep, or her peace of mind. She should be relieved that he'd suddenly lost interest in her. That's what she'd wanted, and it meant she'd have her nice, uncomplicated life back again. For some reason, the prospect wasn't all that attractive.

* * *

"With only ten women in a group of some forty men, Harve had to get lucky," Logan groused. His mood didn't improve at the sound of a deep, masculine chuckle accompanied by a high-pitched giggle in the room behind him. He closed the door, shivering in the cool night air. Harve had been patient enough to let him pull on his clothes and grab his bag.

He looked around the parking lot that was as quiet as a graveyard. There wasn't a light on anywhere in the Cozy Grove Motel, except for three parking lot lights that hadn't burned out. Leaning against the porch post, he stared morosely at the Winnebago where it stood out among the other parked vehicles. All his good intentions had gone for naught. He wasn't about to wait outside until Harve and his lady friend were done, and he wasn't going down to the headquarters room when he had the keys to the motor home in his pocket.

He could sleep in the captain's chair, he decided, crossing the pavement that separated him from the one place he really wanted to be. But he had to think this out. The floor plan was clear in his mind. He'd simply go in, let his eyes adjust to the darkness, walk over to the chair, then settle in for the night. Tory wouldn't even know he was there until morning. Looking at his watch, he amended that to a couple of hours.

The door opened without a sound and he stepped into the Winnebago, carefully pulling the door shut and locking it. He could hear Tory's deep breathing, assuring him she was asleep as he turned in the direction of the chair. His first step brought him up short, his shin connecting with the side of the bed and knocking him off balance. His flailing hand grasped soft, feminine skin instead of the mattress as he expected.

Before he could recover from his fall, he was under attack. A face full of cotton pillowcase muffled his yelp of surprise, then suddenly he could breath again. He gratefully sucked air into his lungs. Knowing Tory was winding up for another blow with her down-filled bludgeon, he reached out blindly to avert another attack. It was a mistake. His hand closed over the soft swell of her breast, rather than one of her arms. He hadn't realized she'd risen to her knees.

Beneath his hand Logan could feel her filling her lungs in preparation for what would probably be a bloodcurdling scream. "Tory, it's me, for god's sake."

"So what?" she snarled after a moment's hesitation. The pillow connected with his side, knocking him over into the tangled sheets. She continued to pummel him as he tried to push himself up again. The air was filled with gasps and groans as he barely gained some leverage on the soft cushion, only to have Tory hit him once more. Each time he almost succeeded, his balance was destroyed by another volley.

Finally, frustrated by his inability to move, he changed his tactics. Lying perfectly still, he waited. When the pillow began its next descent, he rolled onto his back and grabbed it, giving it a sharp tug. He pulled it out of Tory's hands. His plan was more successful than he had anticipated.

The pillow went sailing over the side of the bed, and his arms were filled with a furious female, who was cursing a blue streak. He closed the circle of his arms as a safeguard while he caught his breath. Involuntarily, a chuckle of triumph escaped his lips, but it was quickly drowned out by a groan of pleasure as Tory squirmed against him.

"Honey, this isn't going to help at all," he murmured directly into her ear.

"I'm not trying to help, you jerk," she snapped back, still trying to free her arms which he had trapped against her sides. *This fool isn't going to win so easily.*

"Don't say I didn't warn you."

She barely had time to register his warning before she found herself flat on her back, pinned to the mattress by a lean, hard muscled body.

"Will you listen to me? I only wanted—"

"I know what you want. I woke up with your hand snaking up my hip, didn't I?" She couldn't move with his hands shackling her wrists, his hips pushing her lower body into the mattress. She stopped struggling, waiting for him to relax his grip for just a second.

"I just came in to sleep in the chair," he said and gave her the chance she'd been waiting for as he shifted slightly, taking some of his weight off her by bracing himself on his elbows. "Harve brought a guest back to the room."

Tory's answer was a gasp of surprise. She only managed to make her predicament worse. Shifting her hips brought her into intimate contact with his burgeoning desire, with Logan's leg resting between her own. Only the thin barrier of her nylon panties and his cotton slacks separated her from the pulsing heat.

"Let me up, Logan," she demanded, trying to ignore the molten lava that seemed to suffuse her body from low in her abdomen.

"Would you let me explain, please? I didn't intend this to happen." His voice now had an edge to it, although Tory couldn't figure out what he had to be angry about. It was too dark to see his expression. The only light came from the window high above the bed. She was having trouble concentrating with his thumbs stroking the tender skin on the underside of her wrists.

"A likely story. I should've been suspicious when you walked out of here earlier with barely a good-night," she returned, aggravated that her own voice sounded breathless and slightly hoarse. She arched her back in another bid for freedom and immediately regretted it. The swollen peaks of her breasts brushed against the firm wall of his chest, sending a burst of electricity through her, his breath moist and warm on her face. "Did you really think you could sneak back in here and . . . and, have your way with me?"

"Have my what? Are you talking in your sleep?"

Tory couldn't believe it. He was actually laughing at her. His amusement only added to her frustrations. "No, I'm wide awake *now*, thanks to your unexpected visit. I said, have your way with me."

"Okay, Victoria Camille Planchet, if that's what you want," Logan returned, his tone a mixture of exasperation and amusement.

Tory didn't have time to answer, his lips were warm and persuasive against hers. He allowed her to feel his weight again, laying full length along her body. She realized that they fit together perfectly before she gave herself up to the sorcery of his kiss. Anything that felt and tasted this good had to be black magic because it seemed to sap her strength and any further thought of resistance.

He freed her wrists, but she didn't care as his fingers skated over her shoulders and down her rib cage. In response, she threaded her fingers into his golden-brown mane, pulling him closer. Logan slipped one hand under the hem of her nightshirt where it was bunched up at her hip. This time she welcomed the touch of his hand on her flushed skin, trailing sparks of want and need as his palm slid upward. Brazenly, she pressed her aching breast into his palm in hopes that it would satisfy some basic unknown desire for his touch.

Logan groaned against the sweetness of Tory's lips as her fingers fumbled with the buttons of his shirt. He moved to help her, but she pushed his hand away. Then the soft pads of her fingers were running over him, quickly finding his flat nipples, making him wonder if he would explode from the desire he was trying to contain. He wanted to go slowly and gently, but Tory made him experience an urgency that was totally foreign to him. In a matter of seconds, he had her nightshirt off, wanting desperately to feel her delicate breasts naked against his skin.

His urgency was answered by Tory's feverish hands feathering down his back to dip beneath the waistband of his slacks. Lowering his head he sipped and tasted the gentle slope of her breast, feeling almost lightheaded at her small murmurs of approval. He knew he wouldn't be able to last much longer, but he wanted to assure himself that Tory was at the same level of expectancy. His hand was unsteady as it slipped beneath the thin barrier of her panties, quickly finding the moist, warm core of her femininity.

"Logan, please."

The whispered plea took him over the edge of indecision. He rolled to his side without breaking contact with the tantalizing woman in his arms. Together they unfastened his slacks, awkwardly pulling them off in a nonsensical battle of possession for the garment. Fleetingly, Logan wondered what Tory would have to say about the silver envelope he pulled from his pocket, evidence of some forethought on his part, even though he hadn't anticipated needing it so soon.

Then all rational thought was forgotten as he removed the scrap of nylon that was the last barrier between them. Tory felt like she was in a high-speed car racing out of control toward a steep cliff. She was exhilarated by the feeling rather than frightened, opening her arms to Logan's taut, aroused body as he settled between her legs. He entered her slowly, his lips seeking hers, possessing her completely, irrevocably.

He began moving leisurely, but both of them were impatient for the explosive peak of fulfillment. Tory urged his steady movements clutching his firm hips to express her need, meeting each thrust of his hips and tongue as a willing partner in the passionate dance. Her body was straining to reach the pinnacle as she murmured his name in a litany that Logan answered with provocative promises. Suddenly she was there, trembling on the brink of a fantastic discovery.

Her mind and body melted into one mass of trembling reaction to Logan's final thrust as he called out her name in a hoarse voice. Descending slowly from the amazing journey of pure sensation, she cradled his damp head against her breast, tenderly smoothing tendrils of his golden-brown hair away from his temple. Exhausted from the heat of battle and desire, her heavy eyelids drifted shut, a sigh of gratification escaping her kiss-swollen lips.

SIX

Tory sat with her knees drawn up under her chin, glaring at the sleeping man just a few feet away in her bed. Only his profile and the smooth plane of his back were visible above the rumpled sheets. His right arm was flung out to the side, the side of the bed where she'd been sleeping until a half hour ago. He was smiling in his sleep. She didn't want to think about that satisfied smile, or what had made a shambles of the bedding. She had a problem.

The problem looked dignified in his sleep, his profile perfectly etched against the white pillowcase. He didn't look defenseless or innocent, his natural arrogance somehow clinging to him, even when unconscious. How could he sleep at a time like this? Didn't he know that she had a few pithy things to say about what happened last night?

She wasn't going to sit here looking at his perfectly contoured back, remembering that she'd explored and memorized every muscle and sinew during the night. How long was he going to sleep? Surely she hadn't worn him out? Dismissing the last thought as subversive, Tory looked around for something, anything, that would help her. Staring thoughtfully at Ty Daniel's coloring book for a minute, she turned to study Logan's slumbering form once more.

Before she could change her mind, she grabbed the book. Shifting her position and sitting cross legged, she began to methodically tear unused pages from the book. With great deliberation she crumpled each page into a tight ball, all the while promising her absent nephew a new, jumbo-sized book. Once she had a half dozen weapons in her arsenal, she tossed the book aside.

The first paper wad went wide of the target, but the second hit Logan squarely between the shoulder blades. He twitched in response. Tory muttered under her breath and tried again, landing a shot on the bridge of his aristocratic nose. This time Logan muttered. She pitched the rest of her ammunition in quick succession, hitting the desired target each time with more force.

"Damn it, what's going on?" Logan shot upright, shaking his head from side to side like a wet dog. For a minute his features were a mask of confusion, before he rubbed both hands over his face.

"Not a morning person, are we?" Tory asked politely without moving from her seat.

It took Logan a minute to locate her across the compact interior of the motor home. When he discovered her fully clothed figure in the captain's chair, his eyes narrowed. Tory could almost see his mind at work over the implication. She gave him a beatific smile, then waited.

"What time is it?"

Is that the best he can do? Tory was disappointed. She expected something much more original from a man of Logan's experience. "It's about nine o'clock. We need to grab some breakfast, then head for the staging area."

Logan didn't answer immediately. His arms propping him upright, he seemed preoccupied with the litter of paper that now surrounded him. When his wandering gaze discovered his clothes neatly folded at the end of the bed, he cocked his head to the side, giving Tory a veiled look. "Breakfast?"

She met his stare without flinching, determined he wouldn't know that every ounce of her will power was working overtime to keep from looking at his glorious chest. It was one thing to think up snappy repartee when he was asleep, but a totally different matter with him alert and half naked. "You'd better get dressed, if you want to fit in some breakfast." *Please, please, please*, she begged silently. "It's our only meal until early evening."

"Tory—"

She jumped out of the chair, suddenly needing movement. "I'm already done in the bathroom, so you—"

"Tory—"

"We'll grab a bite here at the motel, then go meet the—"

"Tory!" Logan's shout brought her bright chatter to an abrupt end.

Damn it, I almost made it. She stood on the brink of freedom, her hand on the doorknob, listening for any telltale rustling of the sheets behind her. Would he come after her if she made a run for it? She didn't think she wanted to find out if Logan, stark naked, would chase her around the parking lot.

"Tory, we need to talk about last night," he said quietly.

"What about it?" she asked as innocently as possible, still not daring to turn around. She needed more time, maybe fifty or sixty years, before she'd be ready to discuss last night. If she couldn't explain it to herself, how in the dickens was she supposed to discuss it with him?

"We made love last night," he continued, his voice low and huskier than usual, reminiscent of the sensual murmurs of the night.

"Yes, we did," she said matter-of-factly, turning to glance over her shoulder. With her left hand clenched around the doorknob in a death grip, she casually pulled her cap from her jeans pocket with her right hand. Flipping the cap easily onto her head, she pulled the wide bill low over her forehead. Once that was accomplished, she struck a nonchalant pose with one hand on her hip. "We're both adults, and these things happen, Logan."

He didn't answer immediately, but simply ran his eyes over her body from head to toe.

His heated glance felt like a leisurely caress, but Tory willed herself not to move. Just when she was about to scream in frustration, he spoke. "How often do *these things* happen to you?"

Tory desperately tried to think of at least one of her snappy rejoinders from when he'd been asleep. Unfortunately, the sight of Logan's magnificent chest and sleep-tousled hair seemed to kill her inspiration, and somehow "Your mother wears army boots" wasn't quite suitable. She took a deep breath, hoping something appropriate would come out of her mouth. "We both seem to be a little rusty on our morning-after etiquette. Don't you think postmortems take away the spontaneity of the moment?"

"Is that what you're going to call it? Spontaneity? Arkansas is certainly different from Boston," he challenged, but was stopped momentarily by a thump on the outside door.

"Hey, Tory, shake a leg if you want breakfast," came Alf's muffled shout through the metal barrier.

"Be there in a second," she called back, her eyes never wavering from the man on the bed.

"We're going to talk about this, Tory Planchet, maybe not right now, but we'll talk." Logan's voice was dangerously quiet and controlled. "There's something between us, something I've never experienced before last night. You can deny it to yourself, but don't expect me to play the same game. While you southerners are masters of procrastination, we northerners tend to tackle a problem and solve it immediately."

"Do you usually get results with this domineering male routine? Well, let me tell you something, buster, your Yankee manners aren't going to get you anywhere with me," Tory snarled, refusing to acknowledge his husky words about last night. She'd been right all along, there wasn't much difference between Logan and Reed. Both of them were pompous pigs.

"Fight it all you want to, my southern magnolia. Just remember what I learned last night," he paused, and although she knew he was purposely baiting her, Tory waited for the rest. "You kiss like an angel, and you make incredibly delicious sounds of pleasure when I'm inside you."

Tory walked out the door, his last words echoing through her mind. What had she done to deserve Logan Herrington in her life? She wasn't given time to consider the matter as she crossed the pavement and her name was called from two different directions. If she was lucky she'd be too busy the rest of the day to think about Logan, but she couldn't ignore his presence altogether. She'd have to come up with some rationalization for last night before the ride home tomorrow.

Logan might have let her go this morning, but they'd be cooped up in the Winnebago for the long ride home. It wasn't likely he'd let her ride in the back.

"Hey, Tory, Alf says you asked about your friend

riding in the fast sweep car." Tod Blaylock's cheerful voice interrupted her dark thoughts. "If he still wants to go, we're leaving for the staging area in about five minutes."

"Oh, he definitely wants to go, Tod," Tory returned, knowing an evil grin was turning up the corners of her mouth. There was justice in this world after all. "Logan's in the Winnebago, just go pound on the door. He wants to experience as much of the atmosphere of the race as possible."

She headed for the motel restaurant in a much better frame of mind. Logan could make all the fancy speeches he wanted, but they were on her home ground. By tonight he'd have other things on his mind besides sex.

It was after three in the morning when Logan climbed out of Tod's 4 x 4, feeling as if he'd been run over by a freight train—twice. He seriously considered offering all of his H.P.G. stock for a hot bath to take away the aches and pains. Muscles ached that he didn't even know he had until today. Slamming the door seemed the perfect retaliation for being jostled around the back seat all day, until his arm and back protested at the vigorous movement.

First sweep, my foot, he muttered, smiling at Tod and carefully returning the other man's wave. *We didn't drive under sixty-five the entire day*. He wasn't sure what had been worse, taking the racing stages in daylight, when the course was visible; or at night, when every hair pin turn came as a surprise. He'd swallowed about three acres of Oklahoma soil as well. Although the official contestants had every door and window secured against the elements, Tod claimed he felt closer to nature with all windows rolled down.

In the headquarters' doorway, Logan easily spotted the person who was responsible for his wretched condition. She was standing in the middle of a group, talking and laughing, just as she had been every time he'd seen her during the day.

Tory knew without turning her head that Logan was in the hotel room. She'd felt the same tingling under her skin whenever he appeared during the day. He'd never approached her directly, seeming content to linger on the side lines watching her every move. She knew he wasn't going to hang back this time.

"Hey, son, bet you could use this," Alf announced from directly across the circle of people, holding out a foaming glass of beer. "You look like you've been running alongside the car, instead of riding in it."

Logan's hand appeared in Tory's peripheral vision to take the drink. "Thanks. Tod seems to be a fresh air freak and likes to have all the windows down."

Tory peeked to the side, under the concealment of her eyelashes. Logan had his head thrown back, downing his beer in long swallows. His golden-brown hair was tangled and wind tossed and his aristrocratic face was streaked with dirt. The outline of his sunglasses was still evident, giving him the appearance of a very sexy raccoon.

"So, you've survived your first rally in one piece?" Alf questioned when Logan passed his glass back for a refill.

"One piece is still debatable, but I did survive—chalk one up for the Yankee," he acknowledged with a slanted grin of satisfaction. As the rest of the group laughed, his eyes cut to the silent figure beside him. "If I hadn't seen you during the race today, I'd say you never left the motel."

Tory looked down at her clean clothes, suddenly guilty that she'd returned around midnight to shower and change. "I came back to help set up for the party," she explained, letting her gaze stop at the square cut of his jaw. "We expected you back about an hour ago."

"Tod thought he knew a shortcut back from the last stage, and gave us a nocturnal tour of the entire reservation."

"Tod always has a shortcut," Alf announced, "but he got you back before they finished tallying the results."

"They don't have to hurry on my account because I'm going to turn in now," Logan said before tossing off the last of his second beer. He felt a perverse sense of satisfaction when Tory jumped slightly at his words. "I'll see you all in the morning and you can fill me in on the results then."

He turned away to a chorus of goodnights, a smile of achievement curving his lips as his fingers closed around the Winnebago keys in his jean's pocket. That was where he was headed. Tory could make her own plans for the rest of the night, but he was going to get some sleep in a semi-decent bed.

He realized the minute he'd entered the hotel room that a confrontation amid the crowd was pointless. Although his brain wasn't functioning at full capacity, he knew better than to tangle with the lady tonight. Tomorrow they would have hours together on the ride back to Little Rock. He'd take it slow and easy. He wanted Tory in his bed and didn't want to make the wrong move again. He'd blundered too many times already in their short acquaintance.

Ten minutes later he gave an appreciative groan as warm water coursed over his tired body in the small cubicle of the motor home. At that moment he wouldn't have traded the spartan conditions for the best suite at the Ritz Carlton, even if he couldn't turn around in the shower. He could have stood under the weak spray for hours, but he knew he had to keep his advantage. He needed to be in bed before Tory returned.

She arrived about fifteen minutes later, not bothering to mask the noise of her arrival. The door slammed shut with some force, but Logan didn't move. He remained relaxed, his eyes closed and his breathing regulated to simulate sleep. She stomped around the room with unnecessary, violent moves, making him wonder if she was rearranging the limited furnishings. As casually as possible he rolled over onto his back, making sure the sheet remained above his waist. She didn't need to know he was wearing his briefs beneath the sheet. "What's going on?"

Tory jumped at the sound of his drowsy voice, although she'd been making enough noise to wake the entire motel. She couldn't find an extra blanket or even a pillow in any of the storage compartments. Bracing her hands on the kitchenette counter, she turned to face him, and immediately wished she hadn't.

He was reclining on the bed, one arm raised above his head. The single, overhead light threw his bare chest into relief as he studied her beneath half-closed eyelids. She didn't want to speculate about what he was, or wasn't, wearing beneath the sheet. Her subconscious was already replaying tantalizing memories.

"Go back to sleep, Logan. I was just getting ready for bed," she ordered, cursing the words that came out in a whisper.

"I wasn't asleep. There didn't seem much point until you came to bed."

Tory watched in fascination as he ran his left hand over his chest from his collar bone to his stomach. Her heart skidded with every inch of the descent, mesmerized when his fingers came to rest on his taut midriff. Then his words sank into her distracted brain. "What?"

"I figured you'd wake me up when you got into bed," he explained, then yawned before running his hand over his face.

"You think I'm going to get into bed with you tonight?" Tory demanded, telling herself that she had to remain in control. She couldn't afford to lose her temper now, no matter what the provocation. This was what she'd been preparing herself for all day.

"Thanks for the compliment, sweetheart, but I think you're being a little optimistic." He gave her an apologetic smile, and ruefully shook his head. "Even if my mind was willing right now, my body just isn't going to cooperate. Sorry."

Tory was dumbfounded as Logan turned his back on her and pulled the sheet over his shoulder. If he was trying to drive her crazy, he was doing an excellent job. After fretting and worrying all day about what to do about tonight's sleeping arrangements, she never imagined he'd calmly go to sleep. Her first impulse was to stalk over to the bed and give him a good shaking. She realized, however, that would be stupid. This was what she wanted.

Dragging weary fingers through her hair, Tory took a deep breath. She had to think this through. Exactly what was Logan Herrington up to this time? Was this another ploy? He'd been offhand last night, casually saying goodnight, then returning an hour later. A short woofing noise from the infuriating man seemed to mock her suspicions. He'd actually gone to sleep, and was too upper crust to even really snore.

A jaw-popping yawn interrupted her train of thought. Whatever strategy Logan was using tonight, she wasn't accomplishing anything by falling asleep on her feet. She would have to deal with him in the morning, and that meant she needed a decent night's sleep. She couldn't sleep in the chair.

By only removing her shoes and socks, she was ready for bed in five minutes. Tory hesitated at the side of the bed, wondering if she was falling into a trap, but decided she was too tired to care at this point. She'd been up for over eighteen hours.

Staring down at the cotton plaid bedspread, she had a flash of inspiration. She rolled the thin material into a bolster and laid it in the center of the bed, parallel to Logan's back. Satisfied with her handiwork, she gingerly eased herself down onto the mattress. There was a good four inches of space between her and her companion. Closing her eyes, she smiled and relaxed her tense muscles. Logan was under the covers and she was on top. Everything was under control.

"Okay, let's head 'em up and move 'em out," Tory exclaimed as she climbed into the passenger seat of the Winnebago. "I've paid for the gas, so we're ready to roll."

Logan closed his door and gave her a jaundiced look before turning the key. "Now I know you spent most of the day lounging around the motel during the rally. You couldn't be this cheerful after only six hours' sleep. I think I need at least another twelve hours to feel human again."

Biting her lip, Tory occupied herself with unfolding the road map. She'd had very little sleep, her nerves were stretched to the breaking point, and she hadn't had an ounce of caffeine yet. But, she was going to be happy and carefree if it killed her. As far as Logan was concerned, she didn't have a care in the world.

"You definitely aren't a morning person," she said, continuing to study the map, plotting a new route back to Little Rock. She wanted Logan to concentrate on something else besides her. Driving the twists and turns of the Ozarks on a two-lane road through northwest Arkansas should keep him from discussing more personal matters.

Personal matters like why she'd been draped over his body this morning when he woke up.

"What's so fascinating?"

"I'm plotting the scenic route for the ride home. We'll go back by the northern route, although it's much more spectacular in the fall when the leaves are turning." She was starting to babble, but it was for a good cause. "New England has nothing on the autumn colors of the Ozarks, just a better P.R. person."

"Those are fighting words, lady. No one impugns the honor of our trees," Logan shot back, seemingly willing to keep the conversation on safe ground.

Tory slouched down in her seat, relaxing a little, but still on her guard. She couldn't forget opening her eyes an hour ago to stare into Logan's amused, blue gaze, only millimeters away from her own. Sometime during the pre-dawn hours the bedspread had disappeared from between them. Her body had been plastered against Logan's, her fingers stroking his bare arms.

And she wasn't the only one who'd been taking liberties. Logan was a willing participant in the game. His hand was splayed across her rib cage. As her body came fully awake, she realized the heat from his hand was touching bare skin.

Logan flexed his hand against the steering wheel, still remembering the satiny texture of Tory's skin. Damn, he'd been tempted to forget everything and throw caution to the wind. Only the wary look in her eyes kept him from covering her body and seeking her passionate response. Closing his eyes for a moment, he ruthlessly erased the image from his mind. Then, by staring fixedly at the road ahead, he finally managed the Herculean feat.

With a grimace, he realized his uncle would be delighted by the situation. Damned if Preston was going to find out about his difficulties with Tory. The older man already proved he had a perverse sense of humor by setting up this trip. His cup would run over if he ever discovered Logan's inept attempts at seducing his friend's daughter.

"Hey, earth to Logan! Do you want me to drive while you take a nap?"

"Pardon?" The amazement in Tory's voice broke through his distraction.

"I've been explaining the new route to you for five minutes, and you haven't said a word. I thought you might be one of those people who sleeps with his eyes open."

"Sleep? I've heard that word somewhere before," Logan returned, pretending to give the matter serious consideration. Idle conversation might just keep his mind off more dangerous thoughts. "It has something to do with lying down on a soft surface and closing your eyes, doesn't it? I used to do something like that back home in Boston, I'm sure of it."

"Oh, my. This calls for some serious, emergency measures," Tory murmured. "Pull into that parking lot up there on the right."

"What are you planning to do?" he asked suspiciously, but followed her orders and turned into the gravel parking lot. There were a few vehicles parked near the single story, brick building. A simple sign proclaimed Milt and Myrna's Place.

"Administer the proper medication for your condition, caffeine and sausage biscuits."

He was beginning to enjoy himself again. Tory Planchet wasn't just the sexiest woman he'd met in a long time, she was also the most fun. He didn't remember when he'd ever enjoyed talking nonsense so much. "Sausage biscuits?"

"Save me from ignorant Yankees," she exclaimed, throwing her hands in the air and looking up at the roof for some kind of deliverance. "This is a breakfast delicacy, my man. You take a light and fluffy biscuit, warm from the oven, and cut it in half. Then you carefully place a piping hot sausage patty in the middle. Ta da—a sausage biscuit!''

"This isn't one of your Aggie jokes, is it? Don't you people eat things like corn flakes or plain, old eggs and bacon?''

"Trust me, Logan, you'll love it,'' Tory said with confidence, then scrambled out the door. "You have to experience every facet of the South while you're here.''

"I'm beginning to wonder if I'll survive my three months. I'm still trying to recover from experiencing every nuance of yesterday's rally,'' he put in dryly, noting that she had the grace to look slightly chagrined. Tod Blaylock had told him about Tory's rationale for placing him in the fast sweep car.

"Well, as I was saying, the sausage biscuit is a regional delicacy that needs to be experienced in the pure form,'' she continued as they entered the restaurant, using her best tour-guide tone. "There's a fringe element that claims it has to be drowned in milk gravy to be palatable.''

"Milk gravy?'' He wasn't sure his stomach was going to handle southern cuisine so easily this morning.

"Relax, I'm from the purist group. Milk gravy only goes on biscuits *sans* sausage, mashed potatoes, or chicken fried steak,'' Tory assured him. "I give you fair warning—never eat breakfast with Curtiss. He puts gravy on everything, including his scrambled eggs.''

"Howdy, folks, I'm Milt. What can I get ya?'' asked a stout man. He looked like he belonged behind the wheel of a semi, except for the butcher's apron that was wrapped around his generous waist.

"We'd like two orders of sausage biscuits, no gravy, and lots and lots of hot coffee,'' Tory ordered without consulting Logan.

"Right away. You just passing through?" Milt asked with a friendly grin.

"We're on our way back to Little Rock from the car rally at Grove," Tory answered, her smile matching his. "Is this your place?"

"That's me, one half of Milt and Myrna. The little woman is in the back cooking. You're in for a real treat with her homemade biscuits."

"Then you'd better get back here and give their order, you old fool," interrupted a gravelly voice from the end of the room. A woman who matched Milt pound for pound stood in the doorway that led to the kitchen. "Leave those folks alone and fetch their coffee."

Milt was off in a flash, moving rapidly for a man his size, but not before giving Logan a masculine look of resignation.

Watching Tory glance around the unimposing decor of the restaurant, Logan made a decision. He needed to know when he would hold her in his arms again. She might not speak to him for the rest of the trip, but she wasn't going to run off when he had the keys to the Winnebago in his pocket.

"I'll eat sausage biscuits on one condition," he began, speaking slowly to make sure he had her attention before he forged ahead. When Tory turned to face him, her brown eyes were wide with innocent curiosity. He almost swallowed what he was going to say, but forged ahead. "If we talk about what happened the other night, I'll eat my breakfast without a single complaint."

Tory was saved from answering by Milt's return with a thermal carafe of coffee. She gave the man a weak smile, wishing she could sink gracefully under the table and disappear. Just when she thought everything was going so smoothly, Logan had to ruin everything. So much for her plan to distract him with a difficult drive.

"Well?" Logan prompted after Milt went back to the kitchen.

"Logan, what's the point in dredging all this up again? We made love, it was nice and it won't happen again." Tory was proud of her control, her tone was calm and reasonable. He couldn't know that her pulse was doing a two-step and that her palms were sopping wet.

"It was *nice*?" Indignation radiated from every inch of his body.

How was she going to get herself out of this one? Why did she always make a fool out of herself with this man? It was bad enough that he was determined to discuss their lovemaking. Now she had wounded his ego. Why couldn't he have stayed in Boston where he belonged?

Boston. The word was an inspiration. Logan wasn't the only who was going to get some answers. Repressing a triumphant smile, Tory quickly rehearsed her question, making sure that she had it just right.

"Tory, you can't ignore what happened forever. This is—"

"I'll be glad to discuss it on one condition."

The startled look on Logan's face was priceless. Tory could feel her lips twitching. He had that startled look that was so reminiscent of Ty Daniel caught in the act. Apparently he'd been prepared for a long, drawn out argument.

"What's the condition?" His eyes narrowed in a speculative look. Now that his initial shock had passed, he clearly didn't trust her.

"You tell me why you're in Arkansas."

The statement hung between them. If she didn't know better, Tory would have sworn Logan was squirming in his seat. He wouldn't look at her, showing more interest in the pattern he drew on his paper placement with his fork.

"Here ya go, folks. Myrna's sausage biscuits straight from the oven," Milt announced innocently. The atmosphere between Tory and Logan, however, was easy to read as he set down their plates. He leaned toward Logan, and after a quick glance over his shoulder at the kitchen, informed the other man, "Son, whatever it is, just apologize. Doesn't matter if you're right or wrong, you've got to be the one to apologize. It makes life much easier that way."

Tory picked up one of her biscuits and bit into it as she waited for Logan's answer. He looked at the kitchen door where Milt had disappeared, then slowly turned back to face Tory. Although she couldn't identify the expression in his eyes, she suddenly had a lump in her throat. For a moment, she considered retracting her question.

"You drive a hard bargain, sweetheart," Logan finally managed. He still needed to take a deep breath before he continued with his confession. Once he began, the words tumbled over each other. "My uncle decided that I didn't have any emotions, or at least not enough for a relative of his. I've been exiled to Arkansas for three months to learn how to be a human being, instead of a preppy android. There, are you satisfied now?"

Tory was appalled. How could Preston Herrington do this to Logan? After his explanation, she knew what the unfathomable expression was in Logan's eyes. He was hurt and bewildered by his uncle's action. Preston might have a point in sending Logan south, but he apparently hadn't handled the situation with much finesse.

Yes, Logan was slightly arrogant and too demanding at times, but he certainly wasn't an android. She hadn't made love to an animated computer; he'd been a passionate, virile male. As far as she was concerned, Logan was a little too human, but she wasn't going to admit that to him.

"Just how is Arkansas supposed to help your . . . condition?" she asked hesitantly. The conversation about their lovemaking might have been safer after all, she decided after a moment's consideration.

"My uncle thinks that exposure to your family is a step in the right direction. He's made a living codicil to his will that keeps me out of H.P.G., if I don't come home cured." Logan grimaced at the statement, and picked up a sausage biscuit almost without realizing it. He took a bite and seemed surprised that he liked it. "Your father is to act as my guardian, overseeing my progress."

"I'm surprised you didn't run screaming back to the airport the minute you laid eyes on T.L."

"I gave it some thought," he admitted with a slight smile, "but Herringtons are made of stern stock. We persevere under the most arduous conditions; it's our Pilgrim heritage."

The level look he gave Tory reminded her of how the conversation began. Damn, he was persistent. He'd met her condition and expected her to honor her part of the bargain. She wasn't about to sacrifice herself to a quicky affair to help Logan mark time in Arkansas.

"Don't get your hopes up, mister. I'm not going to jump back into bed with you to help you prove that you're human," she said boldly, not trying to sugar coat her refusal. "I don't indulge in short-term affairs. What happened the other night was an accident. I can't explain it any better, but it won't happen again.

"I'll be glad to help you meet Preston's stipulations, but only if you keep your hands to yourself. I won't be your lover, but if you need a friend, I'll be glad to help." She took refuge in eating the rest of her breakfast. Her speech had been perfect—rational and adult. Still congratulating herself, she took a sip of coffee.

"Fat chance."

She almost spewed coffee all over the table and at Logan and his muttered words.

His smile was almost feral. Tory knew she wasn't going to like what else he had to say, and she didn't.

"My sweet, innocent Tory," he began, giving her a condescending, pitying look that she wanted to slap off his face. "There's a chemistry between us that has nothing to do with friendship. I can't be in the same room with you for more than a half hour without wanting to make love to you, and I think you feel the same. Do you really think you can stay out of my bed during the next few months?"

She didn't dare answer him. She couldn't trust herself to open her mouth to deny or confirm anything. Her temper was heating up, but she wasn't sure exactly why she was angry. Was it his arrogant disregard for her feelings, or the shiver of excitement she felt under his heated gaze? If it was possible, she'd hitchhike back to Little Rock. That couldn't be any more dangerous than close confinement with Logan for the next four hours.

"Okay, play it safe for now. I'll try to be the little gentleman, but don't be surprised if I suddenly make a grab for you. Even Bostonians have been known to crack under extreme pressure." All signs of hurt and confusion were gone from Logan's face. His slate-blue gaze was lovingly moving over her face and upper body. The sparkle of amusement was what made her uncomfortable, not the masculine appreciation in his look.

"Just pay the bill, Logan," she muttered, tossing down her napkin and standing up. The rumble of raised voices could be heard from behind the closed kitchen door. Myrna's voice was louder and more forceful than

Milt's. "I'll meet you outside in a few minutes. I think I need to get a few pointers from Myrna on how to handle a man."

Logan's delighted laughter rang in her ears as she walked toward the restroom. Let him laugh now, she thought with a disgruntled sniff, but he wouldn't find her so amusing when she got done helping with his cure. Slapping her hand against the restroom door, she began formulating just the right treatment for transforming a preppy android into a human being.

SEVEN

"Hmmmm."

"Ah-hah."

"Ooohhh."

"Mmmmmm."

Tory's murmurings echoed around the interior of the gazebo, and Logan knew he wasn't going to be able to stand it much longer. For two days he'd been on his best behavior, playing by Tory's rules, but not for much longer. There was only so much a man could take.

Over breakfast Tory announced her brilliant idea on how to help him become more human for Preston. She was going to give him a quiz on his lifestyle. Like a fool he'd agreed. The dumbest moment in his life, except for confessing why he'd come to Arkansas.

"Ah, yes."

Logan threw down his sandwich, kicked back his chair, and reached across the table to snatch the three pieces of paper that she was reading. This nonsense had gone far enough. Tory tried to grab the papers back, but he held them out of reach, his height and the round, metal table hampering her attempts.

"Watch it, you're going to spill the ice tea," Logan warned above the sound of rattling dishes, before steadying the pitcher with his free hand. His rescue didn't stop him from keeping the papers out of her flailing hands.

Perhaps now that he had her attention he could break through the impersonal reserve she'd assumed since their return from Oklahoma. Her attitude was grating on his nerves more than anything else. She claimed she was going to be his friend, but he was tired of being treated like an inanimate object studied under a microscope. He almost wished she wasn't speaking to him again—that showed some emotional involvement— instead of this impersonal niceness.

"Give it back, then. I haven't finished checking your answers," she complained. After another fruitless try, she sat down abruptly and folded her arms over her chest.

"You've been reading this rag for a half hour, hemming and hawing and smirking," he shot back. With deliberate movements, he bent to pick up his chair and sat down slowly, keeping his eyes on Tory every second. "If I'd known you were a closet Sigmund Freud, I'd never have agreed to this. What is this? Bait-a-Yankee week? And to think I was beginning to enjoy my visit to Arkansas."

"You're just over sensitive about this. I was simply studying your answers for a thorough analysis." She glared at him, thrusting out her lower lip.

Lord, she wants me to think of her as a friend, and all I want to do is kiss her, Logan groaned to himself, focusing on the rounded curve of her pouting lip. *I'm furious with her, but I still want to make love to her*. Somehow, although she was dressed in a cotton T-shirt and jeans, he was struck again by the impression that she should be wearing lace and ribbons. "I am not over sensitive; I'm impatient and bad tempered. Didn't your thorough analysis tell you that?"

"It's nothing to brag about. What you need to do is learn how to relax," she stated smugly. Dropping her militant pose, she reached for her chicken salad sandwich, chewing thoughtfully before she continued. "I think that might be the point Preston was trying to make in sending you here. A little rest and relaxation, you know. Learning to be a little more laid back."

"I might consider wearing suspenders, nothing garish, but I draw the line at a cap. I don't wear hats." Yes, things were progressing fairly well, he decided. Tory's face was flushed and her eyes gleaming with life again. She was starting to forget her mannequin-like pose in the heat of discussion.

"What are you talking about?" Tory's forehead creased slightly as she frowned in confusion.

"When you said laid back, T.L. rocking on the back porch immediately came to mind. I don't think I'm cut out to be a full-fledged southerner," Logan returned, giving her a doleful smile. "I'd never be able to hold my head up at the club."

"I wasn't thinking anything that drastic, so you can preserve your image. But you do need to adjust your thinking a little." She pushed her plate to the center of the table and leaned her elbows on the table. Cupping her chin in her palms, she studied him for a minute. "That list you have in a death grip was very revealing."

Logan looked down in surprise at the papers that were still clutched in his fist. He laid them on the table, pressing out the wrinkles with the palm of his hand. The action kept him from thinking about Tory's cleavage, suddenly more prominent at the top of her scoop-necked T-shirt as she leaned forward. He had to keep his mind on the business at hand, not on remembering how Tory looked without a stitch of clothing, or how the satin texture of her skin felt under his hand. His dreams had been haunted by her for two nights, and the smell of jasmine perfume was driving him nuts.

Clearing his throat unnecessarily, he asked, "Just what did you discover, Dr. Freud?"

"Cute, Logan. You don't do anything for fun. Every activity is work oriented, either at the office or at social functions. You spend more than forty hours a week at the office," she explained, starting to count off the activities on her fingers. "You go to the theater or the opera, but it's for fund-raising projects. Every dinner you've listed is with your mother or uncle with his wife along, again for H.P.G. functions or charity. Your dates seem to be business associates or relatives of business associates. The only recreational activity seems to be your health club. And you're worried about holding your head up there?"

"That's crazy," he shot back, ignoring her caustic jibe. When Tory simply raised her eyebrows and pointed to the list, he was forced to pick up the rumpled papers. He looked at his answers from her point of view. Galling as it might be, he had to admit she was right. How had his life become so dull?

"Okay, let's take another tack," Tory announced after a few minutes. "If you were in an elevator with three other people, a man and two women, what would you do when the doors opened?"

"Is this one of those trick questions? You're not going to ask me about the color of a bear passing the window, or who lies in the house next door to Mr. Green, are you?"

"Pardon?" Tory gave him a quizzical look, then seemed to understand his question. "Oh, those silly logic problems. No, this is just idle curiosity from my experiences visiting the North."

Logan stood up and began pacing in the small space

allowed by the octagon structure. This was something important to Tory, so he had to be careful with his answer. She had the strangest thought pattern of any woman he'd ever encountered. Others had questioned him about when the Herrington family settled in the Massachusetts Bay Colony, or the exact net worth of H.P.G. in round figures. The elevator question was definitely a new approach, or was it?

"Well, I'd get out of the elevator, if it was on the floor I wanted," he finally managed, almost making it sound like a question.

"Uh-huh." Tory nodded slowly, seeming to analyze this bit of trivia the same way she had his list of answers. "Okay, if you saw that a person had a flat tire near you in a parking lot, what would you do?"

"Feel sorry for them I suppose," he answered, still hesitant. He couldn't figure out where she was heading, but he wasn't about to admit he'd never changed a tire in his life and wouldn't know what to do if he had such a problem.

"Uh-huh." The little furrows in Tory's forehead deepened as the corners of her mobile mouth dipped downward.

"Is there a reason behind all this?" Logan felt compelled to ask at this negative omen. The conversation was completely out of control. He wasn't used to being the one ill at ease. He was accustomed to having the upper hand, being in control.

"I was curious about the difference in attitudes between your environment and mine." She gave a careless shrug that made him feel more restless, and he continued his pacing.

"I get the impression that you weren't suitably impressed," he remarked, trying to appear nonchalant. This obsession she had about the difference between

North and South didn't bode well for furthering their relationship. He had to show her it was ridiculous.

Tory shrugged again, tilting her head to the side to watch his restless strides. "It's nothing personal. I was simply testing a theory. Hardly anyone in the North seems to hold doors open anymore, as well as forgetting a few other niceties while they're rushing around at hyper-speed. Everyone's too preoccupied with their own business to take the time to remember common courtesy. Do you know that last week when I had a flat tire downtown, three men I'd never met before argued over who was going to change my tire for me?"

"How nice." He gave her what he thought was a noncommittal smile, but it had Tory looking at him strangely. He clenched his jaw, hoping she wouldn't notice the telltale sign of his precarious control. No one questioned a Herrington's upbringing, especially an opinionated young woman who went out of her way to find fault with anything that came from above the Mason-Dixon line. After all, his family was eating off crystal and china while her ancestors were probably still scouring the woods for beavers and raccoons as fashionable attire.

"Aren't you being a little judgmental about someone you've known for a short time? I could make a few sweeping accusations about you, with the same limited knowledge," he finally managed in a suppressed growl, wondering how one woman could make him experience desire and anger at the same time. He glared at her for good measure, standing at his full height with his hands on his hips.

"Such as?" Tory asked with a mixture of confidence and wariness in her expression that told Logan he'd finally shaken her out of her earlier mood. Schooling his features to maintain a placid expression, he continued, "You live rent free on your father's property, drive a succession of borrowed classic cars, and seem to have plenty of spare time on your hands. What do you think I would assume from all that, Ms. Planchet?''

His smile was a masterpiece of superiority, one he'd used for years at restaurants with inferior food and poor service, or anytime he held the upper hand. When she didn't answer immediately, he gave her his summation. ''I see a person with no real responsibility passing judgment on me. Like I said, you live rent free, have your meals prepared for you, drive a fleet of expensive cars, and have a nice little hobby in catering, but you think I need some lessons on how to live. Fascinating.''

Tory gave him a level stare, meeting his accusing look with placid maple eyes showing no sign of irritation. ''Now that you've got that out of your system, can we get back to the main topic of discussion?''

''Has anyone ever threatened to strangle you?'' he asked earnestly, but he could feel the tension leaving his body. For some unknown reason, he suddenly had to keep himself from smiling at her.

''Most of the time it's not strangling. My brothers and T.L. seem to think a hickory switch does the trick,'' she answered honestly, a smile turning up the corners of her mouth.

''I'd stay out of New England, if I were you.'' He unbent enough to return her smile.

Giving him a guileless look, she asked, ''Why is that?''

''They'd probably bring back burning witches at the stake, just in your honor.''

''Then it's a good thing I don't plan to leave Little Rock anytime soon.'' She got to her feet, rubbing her palms against her jean encased thighs. ''We need to get these dishes cleaned up before we go shopping.''

''Shopping?'' He couldn't figure out where this was going to lead, but he wasn't going to lose his temper again. He'd play by her rules for now, staying calm and collected. Nothing was going to upset him.

"This ne'er-do-well has to go to the grocery store and buy supplies for the party she's catering Saturday night on the *Spirit*. So we're going to the grocery store to give you another experience at the unknown," she explained, while gathering up the remains of their lunch.

"The *Spirit*?"

"A riverboat on the Arkansas River, and it's scheduled for a retirement party." Tory picked up Logan's questionnaire and carefully folded it before putting it in her hip pocket. He couldn't resist watching her slide the paper into the snug material, then tried to look innocent when she caught him staring.

He smiled at her and took the tray, waiting patiently for her to load it with their dirty dishes. This was something the true southern gentleman would do, wasn't it? Staring at the roof line of the gazebo should keep him out of trouble for the next five or ten minutes.

Yes, pushing a shopping cart around the grocery store should get Logan's mind off my body, Tory decided, thankful his questionnaire was helping her keep her mind off his. The man actually had his groceries delivered, and a housekeeper who did his cooking. And he thought she had no responsibilities.

Tory studied Logan's profile, thrown into stark relief by the sunshine that outlined his lean frame. He'd looked magnificent a few minutes ago when he glowered at her. She felt a twinge of regret. This wasn't the quiet, sensitive man she was looking for to fill the empty spaces in her life. After Reed, she'd evaluated exactly the type of man that would fit into her life. A stubborn, self-possessed Yankee didn't fit the pattern she'd designed, no matter how tempting his amazing chest, or how compelling his elusive smile.

Her tactic to defuse his anger had worked perfectly.

He was still sensitive about being sent to Arkansas, so anything she said was bound to set him off. They were on safe ground as long they didn't talk about sex or Logan's family. She planned to steer clear of anything that even looked controversial. She wasn't about to be the one on the defensive. Whenever she lost her temper, she always got in trouble, or landed in Logan's arms, which was the same thing.

If she hadn't realized it before, reading his answers confirmed that the man wasn't interested in commitment or emotional responsibility. To Logan, an affair was simply a means to satisfy his physical needs, his emotions weren't involved. It was apparent in the way he went from hot to cold. One minute he was logical and composed, the next he was angry and passionate. Unfortunately, he was calm and calculating in his pursuit of her, not the victim of his emotions.

Why did she offer to be his friend? It was probably the dumbest thing she'd done in her entire life, except maybe letting T.L. talk her into being nice to Logan. She couldn't wait for the old goat to get back from Texarkana and take Logan off her hands.

Her mind kept betraying her at the oddest times. Like right now as she allowed Logan to walk ahead of her toward the house. An image of Logan lying in bed wearing nothing but a smile flashed across her mind. Shaking her head, she began reciting her menu for the Ferguson retirement party and compiling her grocery list. The ingredients for Caesar salad and pecan tarts had to take her mind off how well Logan Herrington filled out a pair of slacks.

"Do I have to talk to the girl behind the popcorn counter about her personal life?" Logan asked above the noise of the theater lobby a few days later. He looked around him in horrified fascination at the jumble of arms and legs, and the piercing voices of the children attending the five o'clock movie. Ty Daniel and Amanda Sue stood next to him, clinging to Tory's legs as they stood in the concession line.

"No, I think it's too crowded for a lengthy conversation," Tory admitted, biting back a smile, "but don't forget to say, yes, ma'am or no, ma'am." Over the past few days she had been demonstrating a laid back approach, showing him how to interact with the people in the grocery store and in two restaurants. He'd heard about the grocery clerk's forthcoming gall bladder operation, looked at the pictures of one waitress's grandchildren, and knew every detail of another waitress's doomed love life. He'd been amazed that Tory hadn't known any of these people beforehand. It just wasn't done that way in Boston.

But that was the only comment he'd made. He'd gotten through each experience without a single objection. It worried her. He held the door open for her wherever they went, pulled out her chair, and always stood when she or another woman entered the room. And although she should be happy with the progress he'd made, she was uneasy.

"Logan, I'll take the kids over by the theater entrance while you fetch the goodies. Remember, one Big Bomber buttered popcorn, a small box of regular popcorn, two small drinks—orange and grape—a medium diet cola, and whatever you want to drink. They'll give you a box, and we'll needs lots and lots of napkins."

She led the children away, trying not to snicker at the stunned expression on Logan's face. What she was doing was really rotten, but Logan needed more exposure to the real world. There wasn't anything more real than going to the early showing of a Disney movie. Fleetingly, she wondered if Logan had ever seen a Disney movie, even as a child.

He'd agreed to the expedition without a quarrel, but he'd only seen Curtiss's kids over dinner when they were out numbered three-to-one by adults. So far, Ty Daniel and Amanda Sue had been angels, but they could turn into demons at any time. Then she'd see if Logan was really learning anything.

It didn't take long for the children's transformation to take place. Logan herded them into the theater and found them seats, still looking a little shell-shocked from the concession stand.

"No ice," Amanda Sue snapped, pushing her grape drink at Logan, who was sitting between her and Ty Daniel. She'd waited until the opening credit of the movie to start her protest.

"It has ice," Logan whispered helpfully, prying back the top to show her.

"No ice," she repeated louder than before and pushed at the cup, splashing grape drink on his beige twill slacks.

"Oh, dear, I forgot," Tory began contritely because she'd forgotten about the child's dislike of ice. She almost choked on her words at the accusing look Logan gave her. "She doesn't like ice in her drink. Give it to me, and I'll take it out."

"Shhhhh," hissed a voice from behind them as Tory awkwardly made the transfer. She was thankful that the theater used ice cubes instead of crushed ice.

With the ice situation handled, they settled back to watch the opening credits. The minute the movie started in earnest Ty Daniel spoke up, at the top of his lungs, "Logan, I have to pee."

Tory's heart almost melted at the stunned look Logan gave her. She'd volunteer to take her nephew, but it would only create a scene. Ty Daniel was into a macho stage, refusing to be taken into the women's restroom. She just shrugged when Ty Daniel tugged on Logan's sleeve and proclaimed his need again. This was a situation that she hadn't anticipated.

"For heaven sakes, mister, take your kid to the restroom," demanded the same voice from behind them.

A half hour later, when Logan hadn't returned with his charge, Tory was about to send out a search party. She wasn't sure who she'd be rescuing—Logan or Ty Daniel. Just as she was getting to her feet, the shuffling at the end of the aisle caught her attention. Logan was carrying Ty Daniel by his arm pits, holding him out in front of him as he worked his way to their seats. After tossing Ty Daniel, who was happily sucking on a red licorice whip, into his seat, Logan met Tory's wide-eyed look over the boy's head. He gave her a semblance of a smile, really more a grimace, before slouching down into his seat.

Although he didn't seem to be too angry, she knew that she was going to pay for this. It seemed like such a good idea this morning when Leeanne called to remind her of her promise to treat the kids to the Disney movie. Sneaking another look at Logan, she slunk down into her seat as Amanda Sue began quizzing Logan about every minute detail of action on the screen.

"Does your sister-in-law ever talk?" Logan asked in the blessed quiet of Tory's car. They'd delivered the *Children from Hell* to their parents, staying to have coffee with Curtiss and Leeanne after the little ones had been hosed down and put to bed. He was surprised to discover that he missed the children's chatter during the quiet, adult conversation. Especially after both Ty Daniel and Amanda Sue had hugged him goodnight and thanked him for taking them to the movie.

"Of course, she talks," Tory answered absently, "Why?"

Logan smiled under the cloak of the dark interior of the car. Tory had been wary of him since they'd left the theater. She'd spent most of the visit at her brother's house eyeing the grape drink stain on his pants and the licorice smears on his shirt. When he'd laughingly explained the mishaps to Curtiss and Leeanne, Tory looked at him as if he were a ticking bomb.

"I thought I might have done something wrong. I seem to make her nervous," *and she isn't the only one*, he finished silently.

"She's shy and gets nervous around strangers sometimes, so she defers to Curtiss quite a bit," she explained, seeming to come out of her abstract thoughts. "Leeanne's very sweet and a wonderful mother."

"I wasn't criticizing her. I was just curious." Logan thought over the matter for a minute. "You seem a little defensive about my comment."

Tory braked for a red light and glanced in his direction. "I'm sorry. This is something my other sister-in-law loves to harp about."

"But I don't remember that she was all that talkative the night I met your family."

"Exactly. For different reasons, my sisters-in-law let their husbands take center stage." Her voice was shaded by disdain as she accelerated through the intersection. "Leeanne's shyness keeps her from speaking to strangers, and Adele thinks that the man of the house—in this case Sanders—always has more interesting things to say."

"Are we a little militant on the subject of marriage?" Although he was teasing, Logan really wanted to know the answer.

"Not really. Just on women who become idiots when they get married. Adele was a very successful realtor before she married Sanders ten years ago. She's well read, well traveled, and a witty conversationalist—until she's with my brother." Tory couldn't keep the anger out of her voice. "Leeanne has always been shy, and

unfortunately, Curtiss takes advantage of the fact sometimes. He lets her wait on him hand and foot, knowing
she's not going to object.''

"I think you should meet Uncle Preston's wife, Babs.
She'd restore your faith in the sanity of married women,''
Logan declared, unable to keep the amusement out of
his voice.

"Logan, I'm serious about this. Abby Bush is another prime example. I swear that she hasn't made a
move outside the house by herself since she married
Gary last year. He even drives her back and forth to
work every day.'' She slapped her hand against the
steering wheel to emphasize her point, getting into the
spirit of her monologue. "This is a woman who's been
my second-in-command for three years. I could always
depend on her if I couldn't be there to supervise a job. I
made her a manager of my West Little Rock shop, but I
wonder if she's going to be able to make a decision
without checking with Gary first.''

"Bet you can't name four?'' Logan challenged.

"Name four what?'' Tory stopped at the gate to
punch in the security code.

"Name four wives who are walking dishrags,'' Logan continued, as she steered the car through the gate.
For some reason her attitude towards marriage bothered
him. Maybe it was because it seemed at odds with her
usual optimistic outlook.

Tory didn't answer, letting the silence continue until
she stopped the car near the back of the main house.
She didn't wait for him to come around the car to open
her door. When Logan rounded the front of the car she
was standing with her hand resting on the open door.
"You know, I can't think of a fourth wife, but three out
of four isn't very good odds.''

"You definitely need to meet Babs to restore your
faith in the institution of marriage,'' he commented,

taking her arm and leading her toward the cottage. "She's a photojournalist. Now, she did change her assignments after she got married, so she didn't end up in Europe when my uncle was assigned to a story in the Philippines. Of course, she only freelances now that Uncle Pres is back in the States for good."

"That makes sense. You do have to compromise in a relationship, but one person doesn't have to make all the sacrifices," Tory decided. Suddenly she stopped on the path to her cottage, realizing where she was. She looked up at Logan in confusion, her face clear in the moonlight. "What are you doing?"

"Walking you home like the courteous gentleman that I am," he explained, wondering why he hadn't just gone in the house. The minute he touched her, even an impersonal hand under her elbow, and his hormones started raging out of control. He hadn't wanted the evening to end just yet, reluctant to break off their conversation.

Now he knew it was a bad idea. The soft breeze coming from the river, a full moon, and not a soul in sight intensified his desire to hold Tory in his arms. There was something intrinsically feminine in the way she moved, no matter what she wore. The simple blouse and skirt she wore clung to her rounded figure, weakening his defenses without any overt signal from Tory.

"Why does it make me nervous that you're adapting to the southern way so easily?" Tory asked the question reluctantly, unwilling to break the accord between them. But she had to know if he was just playing a game.

"Do I make you nervous? You don't like it that a Yankee can be adaptable?" Although she couldn't read his expression, his predatory grin taunted her.

She closed her eyes for a minute, letting his husky voice wash over her. When she opened her eyes, he seemed to be standing closer. "I don't think I trust you, Logan."

"Maybe you don't trust yourself," he replied, his voice soft and seductive, daring her to deny his statement.

It wasn't her imagination—the space between them had diminished to less than an inch. Tory began walking backward, one cautious step at a time. Her retreat did little good since Logan matched her step for step, his hand trailing down her arm to clasp her hand.

"Logan, let's not complicate this anymore than necessary. I'm not going to become involved in an affair that will end when you return to Boston." Her voice trailed off and the tentative smile with which she tried to lighten the sudden tension in the air faded when Logan moved toward her again. "We need to keep this at the friendship level, plain and simple."

"Sweetheart, nothing has been simple from the moment I saw you at the airport," he stated in a low drawl at the same moment Tory's foot slipped on the flagstones. Logan was more than willing to help her regain her balance, raising his hands to grasp her slender shoulders.

Tory didn't believe the fission of excitement that raced up her arms the moment her hands made contact with Logan's chest. After a week of resisting the need to touch him, all she wanted to do for a wild, impulsive moment was melt into the warm shelter of his arms. She wanted to lean forward and press her lips against his chest at his open collar. Involuntarily, she slipped her fingers toward the open triangle, moving her palm against the hair roughened skin, giving in to her need for a single, mad moment.

When Logan murmured his approval deep in his throat, she raised her startled eyes to his face. She was lost. His eyes gleamed in the darkness for a brief second before he lowered his mouth to claim her innocently offered lips. If he'd been demanding or rough, she might have pulled away, but he gently nipped at the corners of her mouth. With each small nibble her level of arousal increased, making her impatient for him to kiss her fully, deeply, but he continued to torment her.

She had the feeling he was tasting her. The intriguing thought made her open her eyes. Logan was watching her as well. Tory hadn't experienced anything like this before. He almost seemed to be daring her to take the initiative. She was aware of her hands sliding over the contours of his chest, although she didn't remember her desire clouded brain making the decision.

As she tangled her fingers in his thick brown hair, Logan finally gave her what she'd been longing for. His mouth slanted over hers, and she parted her lips, willingly accepting the thrust of his tongue. She moved against his lean body to lessen the aching warmth that was beginning to kindle low in her body. The touch of Logan's hand skimmed a trail of fire down her back before he cupped her buttocks, pulling her against his taut desire.

Knowing she was out of control, she was helpless to stop the waves of pure feeling that sapped her resistance. Aware he was dangerous, the pleasure of rubbing her swollen breasts against the hard wall of Logan's chest made her forget any need to escape. She wanted to cry out when he broke the kiss, until his mouth trailed across her cheek to the overly sensitized skin below her ear. He was finding pleasure points that she never knew existed before he came into her life.

"Oh, sweetheart, we're so good together," he breathed into her ear, the words skating down her spine. "I want you, Tory. I want to feel you moving under me again, making those little sounds deep in your throat just before you cry out my name. We're so good together.

"Tell me again that you only want to be my friend,

sweetheart. Tell me that you won't be in my bed again before I go back to Boston.''

She wanted him to stop talking. With each word, sanity began to take hold once more, and she became more and more concerned about the danger of what she was doing. Logan shifted slightly, his hands moving between their bodies, his index finger stroking over her collarbone. She liked the sensation on one level of her mind and on another level an alarm was going off, telling her to break away before it was too late.

The heated touch of his hand against her breast caused her to stiffen, suddenly aware of what was happening, what she was allowing to happen without protest. Fear at how vulnerable she was overruled the sensations of desire that had been blinding her to what she was doing.

"Logan, stop. We can't do this.'' Her voice was unsteady, but it strengthened her resolve. She wasn't going to be a convenient diversion for him during his sojourn to the South. The pain when he left would be too great.

"Tory, what are you saying?'' His words were husky with desire. Raising his head, he looked directly into her eyes, his hand poised at the upper swell of her breast.

"We have to stop. Neither one of us is thinking straight. We have nothing in common except a physical attraction.'' She gained strength as she explained her reasoning, knowing she'd never admit that she'd been so lost in his embrace she hadn't remembered why he was there. All that had mattered was the touch of his hands and the taste of his lips.

"There's nothing wrong with physical attraction. We're both sane, reasonable adults who know how to handle a relationship. You can't tell me you don't want me.''

She flinched at the edge in his voice. Before any softer emotions could overcome her rational mind again, she reached up to pull his hands away from her body. It was still too tempting to give in.

"Tory, we haven't finished this," he warned, but he stepped back, allowing her the freedom to move away.

"All I can say is I'm sorry for letting this get out of hand," she returned, part of her wanting to reach out and comfort him, the other part wanting to run as fast and as far as she could. "I want to be your friend, Logan, that's all."

His harsh laugh sent a shiver of apprehension through her. What had she done by surrendering to her emotions?

"There'll be another time and place, Tory, but not with the same result," he promised. His back was rigid as he turned to walk back to the house. "We are going to be lovers again."

All feelings of compassion flew out of her head at the authoritative statement. Now she knew what had brought her to her senses. It had been the underlying arrogance in Logan's whispered words. She bristled at his conceit. There wasn't a man on this earth who was going to order her around, telling her that she should be his lover no matter what she might have to say about it.

"Let this be your next lesson in southern etiquette," she called after his retreating figure. "Try asking instead of demanding."

She spun on her heels before he could answer, almost afraid he would before she could make her escape. The few steps to the cottage seemed to be endless. With each step she was aware of the man watching her from the end of the walkway. She knew without turning that he'd stopped and was waiting for her to reach the front door.

Logan watched until Tory disappeared inside the cottage. Only then did he slump down on the bench at the end of the walk. He'd never felt as alone in his entire life as he did at this moment. He couldn't be in more pain if she'd slapped him. What he didn't understand was why.

He'd felt desire for other women and been told no at times in the past. Tonight, however, he felt physically and emotionally drained. Why was Tory Planchet getting under his skin like this? Had he been hoping his good behavior would win him a reward? Why did his impassioned words to her sound so hollow? The thought of returning to Boston was losing its appeal. Three months in Arkansas wasn't going to be long enough for him.

Suddenly he was too tired to deal with all the confusing thoughts that were chasing around in his brain. He would do things her way for now, taking it slow and easy. They would play a waiting game. But all the while she was teaching him her brand of living, he would know one important fact: Tory Planchet would be in his bed again.

EIGHT

"So, how's everything going with your gorgeous houseguest?" Abby Bush asked Tory from across the kitchen as she smoothed plastic wrap over a tray of shrimp puffs. They'd been working for four hours on the preparations for the Ferguson party and were almost done.

The question broke through Tory's concentration while she pressed the last cream-cheese rosette for the border around the salmon mousse. The jelled creation was now circled by a garland of rosettes that ended in a gigantic blob. Tory summed up the final product in one succinct word.

"Oh, not so good I see," Abby commented, crossing the room and peering over Tory's shoulder to inspect the damage.

"This party is going to be a disaster, I just know it. Nothing is going right today," Tory announced before tossing the cheese press in the mixing bowl and leaning back against the counter. A tendril of hair fell over her forehead, but with cheesy fingers she could only push at it with the back of her wrist. "So far, we've broken three of our best wine glasses, dumped a quart of fresh strawberries on the floor, and now we have a salmon with a goiter. With such an auspicious start, I don't think things are going to improve."

"Relax, for heaven's sake. You weren't this nervous for your first catering job. We've just had a few minor setbacks," the blond corrected, then pitched a towel across the counter that Tory easily caught. "You've been saying we needed to replace the glasses, most of the strawberries were salvageable, and a spatula will give the salmon a face-lift."

"Do you have to be so agreeable? I was the one who broke the glasses, dumped the strawberries, and trashed the salmon." Tory gave a disgusted sigh and draped the dish towel over her shoulder. With another sigh, she pushed herself up to sit on the counter. "Let's take a break before I destroy anything else."

"Does this mean we get to eat the pecan tart remnants? Huh, huh, can we, Mom, can we, please?"

Tory couldn't keep from smiling at the tall blond down on her knees with her hands clasped in front of her, a pleading look on her oval face. "How many tarts did you break on purpose when you took them out of the tins?"

"You're accusing me of sabotaging the dessert? I'm crushed," the other woman protested as she jumped to her feet. She skipped over to the table and picked up the plate with the tart fragments. Looking back over her shoulder, she confessed, "Only two or three, maybe four. You want ice tea or milk with these?"

"Ice tea, fool."

Tory leaned her head back against the cabinet while the other woman rummaged in the refrigerator, knowing Abby was kidding about the vandalism. She was even more meticulous about waste than Tory.

"Mmmmm, are we fantastic cooks, or what?" Abby

exclaimed a few minutes later, munching on a piece of pecan tart. When Tory didn't answer, she continued, "It's really nice of Arnette to loan us her kitchen during the transition, but I can't wait to get back into the old routine. There's something unsettling about working in a strange kitchen."

"Nice try, but that isn't why I've suddenly turned into a klutzy cook," Tory said dryly, licking the last crumb from her lips. "Not only will we be entertaining the cream of the Little Rock banking community tonight, we'll be under the scrutiny of—What was it you called him? My gorgeous houseguest?"

"Logan is coming tonight?" Although Abby tried to keep her voice level, her raised eyebrows and rounded brown eyes gave away her curiosity. "Don't tell me he won't let you out of his sight? I thought Gary was the only one with an inferiority complex."

"Logan seems to be intrigued by a ride on the *Spirit*. But what's this about Gary? Since when does one of the brightest lawyers in the attorney general's office have an inferiority complex?" She must have misunderstood Abby. Gary Bush was extremely outgoing, and possessed enough self-confidence for a half dozen people.

"Since he married me, apparently. For some reason, he thinks he has to entertain me all the time, take me places, do things together," Abby said, giving a shrug and popping another pecan morsel into her mouth. "Last night I finally had enough togetherness and asked him what was going on. Do you realize I haven't been able to set foot out of the house alone since we were married?"

Tory nodded dumbly, remembering her conversation with Logan the previous night.

"I just don't understand men. Gary told me he didn't want me to become bored now that I was married. He knew that I was always doing something exciting when I was single and didn't think he could compete with my former lifestyle. Have you ever heard anything so ridiculous in your life?"

"It's kind of sweet." The response was weak since Tory felt guilty over her ranting to Logan about marriage making women idiots. Last night she'd been criticizing her friend, and today she was almost envious, wanting someone to care about her that way. Appearances were deceiving, especially when someone came to unfounded conclusions.

"Yeah, it is sweet, dumb but sweet," the blond admitted with an affectionate grin. "After hours of loving attention, I think I finally convinced him that I'm not going to run off with the milkman. It was a tough job, but somebody had to do it."

"Nice work, if you can get it." Tory nibbled on another piece of pecan tart, still a little stunned over misjudging her friend.

"Now that we've dealt with my love life, how about yours, Miss Tory?"

"What love life?"

Abby answered in one word.

"I'm going to talk to your husband about your language," Tory challenged, but knew she wasn't going to be able to avoid talking about Logan much longer.

"You talk to Gary, and I'll have a nice friendly chat with Logan. This is the first guy to have you hot and bothered in a long time, a really long time, a really, really long—"

"All right, all right," Tory shouted. The other woman would keep this up all afternoon and into the night, until she got the information she wanted. Talking to her closest friend might not be a bad idea. "Logan wants to have an affair to pass the time while he's in Arkansas, and I'm the lucky candidate. Or so the dumb Yankee thinks."

"Should I start humming *Dixie* for appropriate background music, or how about *I am Woman*?'' Abby shook her head and gave Tory a reproving look. ''If you met a man who was nice looking, personable, had a good sense of humor, and got along well with your friends, would you consider having a relationship with him?''

''What's the catch?''

''Just answer the question. You haven't dated anyone in over two years, or had a serious relationship since you broke your engagement to Reed.'' Abby paused and waited for Tory to nod in agreement. ''So, I'm giving you a perfectly acceptable example. Would you consider having a relationship with him?''

''I suppose so—''

''Oh, I forgot to mention some minor details,'' Abby broke in, a crafty smile spreading over her face. ''He's fairly assertive, probably as stubborn as you are, and lives in Boston.''

''That's not fair,'' Tory protested.

''What's not fair? You probably had this guy summed up the second you met him, decided he was a clone of the dear, departed Reed, and wrote him off as a nuisance,'' Abby said, ignoring the other woman's protest. ''Reed was a jerk and treated all women like they were second-class citizens. Logan isn't anything like that. He comes across as a fairly reasonable man. Frankly, if I wasn't married, I'd be after him in a second.''

''You've met Logan once, Abby.''

''I'm a quick study; I married Gary six months after we met. Besides, it's clear that the man adores you. I don't know what you argued about before our party, but he looked so lost, watching you from across the room.'' She gave an exaggerated sigh of rapture, pressing her hands over her heart and batting her eyelashes. ''If I hadn't sent Button over to entertain him, you'd probably have ignored him all night.''

"You sicced Button on him? And I thought you liked Logan."

"It's the least I could do to help young love."

"This isn't love, it's lust," *which is the problem*, Tory finished silently with a feeling of depression, and was stunned by the implication of her thoughts. Why would she want Logan to love her?

"Hey, a man can be persuaded to change his mind."

"Hmmm," Tory answered absently, still preoccupied with her own thoughts. She couldn't be in love with Logan Herrington. It was ridiculous. He was the last man on earth who she should love.

"Okay, if that's the way you're going to be, I guess it's back to work," Abby said in disgust. "Where are the extra packing boxes?"

"The boxes?" Tory echoed, then tried to concentrate on the present. "They're on the left top shelf in the pantry."

"This is insane," she murmured the minute Abby left the room. Unable to stand still, she began pacing the length of the kitchen. How could she be so stupid to fall in love with an opinionated, arrogant, ill-mannered Yankee? No matter how much she wanted to deny it, Tory knew that it was true. She'd fallen in love with Logan.

For the life of her, she couldn't figure why, or how it had happened. She didn't have time to reason it out right now. Abby would back any second, and she had an important party to cater. All she felt like doing at the moment was going home, and hiding under the bedspread. That had always been her solution during a thunderstorm, burrowing into the mattress and pulling the covers over her head until the storm was over. Unfortunately, she wasn't a trusting child any more, who accepted love as an uncomplicated emotion.

*   *   *

"Hey, this stuff looks pretty good. I don't think my mother could find fault with this," Logan announced, seeming unduly surprised at the decorative display of food that was being unloaded onto the table in front of him. When he caught Tory's gaze studying him, he frowned and asked, "Do I have a spot on my tie, boss?"

His question caught her by surprise, unaware that she'd been staring at him. He was standing at the end of the long buffet table set up on the main deck of the *Spirit*. Did he have to sound so amazed about the food, and look so handsome at the same time? Was it any wonder she was having trouble concentrating on the job at hand? She'd already forgotten to count the boxes as they were carried onto the boat. "Sorry, I was trying to figure out if all the boxes are here, now that we have the hors d'oeuvres unloaded."

"If they aren't, it's a little late because we've left the dock," Abby announced from behind her. "Don't the boys look nice in their party clothes?"

Logan and Gary linked arms and struck a pose reminiscent of a catalog layout. The two men had volunteered to serve as waiters for the evening when both of Tory's college student helpers called in sick at the last minute. Thanks to Abby's inspiration, they were dressed in matching outfits—charcoal slacks, black vests, and white shirts with a thin, black pin stripe. They complemented Abby's and Tory's gray skirts and maroon vests.

"Give us some straw hats, part our hair in the middle, and we'll sing barber shop, in two-part harmony," Gary announced, an ingratiating smile across his bearded face.

"Just hum under your breath while you work," Tory shot back, trying to count the containers in earnest this time. The guests would be wondering where the food was fairly soon because the boat was underway. Although the weather was perfect with a clear sky and moderate temperature, she was still jumpy. Every guest at Stephen Ferguson's retirement party was influential and could make or break Bill of Fare if something went wrong. There was also Logan's disturbing presence, and the emotions that were lurking in her subconscious.

"Tory, will you relax?" Abby murmured, laying a comforting hand on her arm. "We've done this a hundred times before and for bigger crowds."

"I know, but usually I have a kitchen close at hand and experienced helpers," she whispered back, eyeing the two men at the end of the table. When Logan snitched a marinated mushroom from the perfect symmetry of one of the trays, she groaned, "See what I mean?"

"All right, you two idiots, let's hop to it. You volunteered for this job, and you're going to behave yourselves," Abby exclaimed, pointing an accusing finger at an innocent-looking Logan. When her husband snickered, she turned to glare at him. "Both of you go check the tables and make sure there's enough silverware. When that's done, make sure the wine is iced, and set up the glasses on the table along the railing, then come back for further instructions. This is a first class operation. We don't have time for schoolboy antics, which means the hired help doesn't eat anything until the job is done."

"Yes, ma'am," they agreed in unison, but both men were having trouble repressing their grins.

"Okay, boss, now what?"

"If I don't push one of them overboard before the evening's over, it will be a miracle." Tory watched Logan and Gary wending their way through the maze of tables, still acting like a pair of boisterous adolescents, then shook her head. "Let's take the hors d'oeuvres to the upper deck. They'll need something to nibble on with their drinks. I wouldn't want to be responsible for a tipsy guest going overboard.''

"Tory, will you stop looking for trouble?" Abby asked when they returned from the upper deck. She deftly unpacked the dinner plates and stacked them at the end of the table while Tory began arranging the food for the main course. "We've already had two requests for Bill of Fare's services while we were passing the canapes.''

"That's before they realized we don't have any dessert,'' Tory replied tonelessly from where she stood near the packing boxes. She turned to stare at her friend, a feeling of desperation spreading through her body. "Where *is* the dessert?''

"You have to be kidding. I put the tarts and the ice chest with the fruit in the station wagon myself. They were in the back seat to keep from being jostled.'' Abby abandoned the dishes to join Tory in searching through the boxes and the compact refrigerator. After a thorough search, she sat back on her heels and met her friend's defeated look. "There isn't any dessert, just walnut-banana whip cream for the fruit.''

"Okay, boss ladies, the glasses and wine are all set, what do we do next?" Gary announced from behind them. When neither of the women answered, he looked at his wife closely. "Honey, what's the matter?''

"Do you remember an ice chest and two packing boxes marked dessert?''

"No, I don't think so. How about you, Logan?''

"I didn't look at the writing on the boxes. I just carried them. What's wrong?''

"Unless someone wants to swim back to shore, we don't have any dessert for a party of fifty people,'' Tory groaned. She felt numb inside. In spite of her premonition of disaster, she couldn't believe this was happening. Ironically, despite his earlier amusement, she wanted to seek the shelter of Logan's arms for comfort and reassurance, even if he was the reason for her preoccupation tonight.

As if he read her mind, he moved to her side, curving an arm around her sagging shoulders. "From a conversation I overheard earlier about the river's current, swimming isn't an option. Is there something you can substitute for dessert?"

"Not stranded in the middle of the Arkansas River. I should never have agreed to cater a party on a boat," Tory said numbly, torn between wanting his support and resenting it. This wouldn't be happening if he hadn't come to Arkansas.

"I'll be right back." Logan walked away before the other three could respond.

"How do you tell the president of one of the largest banks in the state that there isn't any dessert?" Tory asked, dreading having to face Tyler Bodine with the news. "Gary, you deal with high-powered types all the time. Any suggestions?"

"Don't give me that, Tory. You've grown up with high-powered types. Bodine isn't going to tear your head off, although he'll probably want a discount," he returned, seeming to be at a loss over how to handle the matter.

"Not if he doesn't know there's a problem," Logan put in as he rejoined the group. He was slightly out of breath, but grinning at the long-faced trio.

"Don't tell me. You told the captain to pull over at the nearest supermarket for frozen yogurt?" Tory asked without enthusiasm. Her whole life was becoming a melodrama. First, she'd fallen in love with the most inappropriate man, and now her business was falling apart before her eyes.

"Not quite, although I did speak to the captain. The *Spirit* has a motor boat, and we should have the dessert on board in about a half hour," Logan announced. When no one responded, he looked around the group expectantly. "Well, who has the keys to the car? It would be a shame to make the trip back and not be able to get to the food."

"I've got them," Tory murmured. She pulled the keys out of her vest pocket and reluctantly handed them to Logan. Why did he have to be the one to come up with a solution? Life just wasn't fair. Here was the perfect situation for her to vent her anger over her tangled emotions, but no, Logan Herrington had to be her knight in shining armor.

"Don't worry about thanking me now, I'll be glad to collect later," he said, his cocky smile not quite reaching his eyes.

He took the keys, but didn't release Tory's hand immediately. She met his hooded gaze, wondering at his hesitant look. When he tugged on her hand, she allowed him to pull her to his side.

"I'll take something on account, just for luck," he murmured and quickly bent his head before she could guess his intent.

His mouth was warm, moist, and possessive. Tory didn't have time to react to the kiss until he was gone. It had taken only a minute, but it shattered the frozen shell she'd built around her emotions. As Logan walked away, whistling under his breath, she wanted to call him back, demanding an explanation. Suddenly she wanted to confront him about the conflicting feelings that had her off balance when she should be thinking about her business, nothing else.

"Gee, do all the waiters get to kiss the boss," Gary asked. His muffled groan brought Tory out of her trance.

Starting in surprise and embarrassment, she realized that she was running her fingers over her lips, as if she was savoring Logan's kiss. She turned to the others to give Gary a withering look, but noticed he was already rubbing his shin. Apparently his wife had already answered his question.

"The only waiter left on board gets to haul the empty boxes and any trash back to the storage closet before the guests come down to dinner," Tory instructed with a smile. The near disaster had shaken her out of her apathy. Now her mind was clear and focused on the Ferguson party. She'd deal with Logan later. "When you get done with that, I'm sure we'll find something even more exciting for you to do."

"What did I do wrong? Were my Yankee manners showing too much?" Logan couldn't contain his curiosity another minute. Although Abby and Gary had done a thorough critique of the successful evening, including the dessert caper, Tory had been silent during the ride back from the dock. She'd remained mute when they stopped at the Bush's house, letting him refuse the invitation to stop for coffee. With the Planchet house in sight, he knew he'd waited long enough to find out what caused her silence.

"Nothing. You saved the evening."

"Why do you sound like that's a crime?" he asked. What was going on here? Tory couldn't still be angry about last night, or could she? She'd been subdued most of the evening, long before the dessert crisis occurred. Apparently he'd lost a major battle with his impatience last night.

"Certainly not. Thank you, Logan, for your invaluable help," she recited, like a child forced to acknowledge a horrible gift from a relative.

"You're in a strange mood tonight."

Tory stopped the car by the back of the house. She put the car in park, then turned to look at him as she turned off the ignition. "I'm always in a strange mood after a near disaster."

"A near disaster that turned into a triumph. Your little dinner was quite a success," Logan corrected. Tory didn't bother to answer and opened her door, not waiting for him to assist her. While he scrambled out of his side of the car, he wondered if he would ever understand women, especially this one. "Bodine was quite impressed with your little business. He was singing your praises to everyone within earshot." She still didn't say a word, so he decided to just keep talking as he came around the front of the car. "In fact, he gave me a twenty-dollar tip. Am I allowed to keep it?"

"No problem," she managed, going to the back of the car and opening the tailgate. "Let's get this stuff unloaded. It's been a long day."

He followed her directions, carrying the empty boxes into the kitchen, still trying to interpret her mood. Maybe she was always this down after a job. The preparation and serving could have sapped her energy level, turning her into a zombie. She'd been her usual sparkling self, however, dealing with her clients. At one point, he thought he'd have to warn off one of Bodine's junior executives when the man spent too much time talking to the owner of Bill of Fare about the food.

"How much work does this usually involve?" he asked, once the boxes were stored in the pantry. Tory was putting away the leftovers, although there wasn't much left.

"It depends on the complexity of the menu. If it's a large group like tonight, I usually manage to convince the client to keep it elegant, but simple." She broke off when Logan reached over to snare a canape before she covered the plate with plastic wrap. "Sorry, would you like something to eat? I wasn't hungry, so I forgot to ask."

He wasn't ravenous, but if it kept her around he'd

eat. "After being tempted all night, I think I might manage a bite or two. Passing out food to other people certainly helps build an appetite."

"It's a good thing I didn't taste this before the party," he managed after munching on a cracker overflowing with salmon mousse. "I wouldn't have let anyone else have any."

Tory rewarded his enthusiasm with a smile. She poured them both a cup of coffee and joined him at the oak table. "Remind me not to have you act as a waiter again. It might be counterproductive to business if you refused to serve the guests."

"You really love what you're doing, don't you?" he asked. Discussing her business was safe ground, he hoped. Although he'd only experienced catering from the clients' point of view before tonight, it might also lead to what was bothering her.

"Yes, I do. Don't you enjoy your work?" She looked intrigued that anyone would pursue a career that they didn't like. Was that why he treated her business as something frivolous?

"I never really thought about it. H.P.G. is the family business, so I've always planned to be part of it," Logan explained, watching her expression with interest. She seemed more relaxed, more animated, since the ride home. She also gave him something to think about. He'd never considered whether he should like his job. It was simply something he always knew he would do.

"Do you have a plan for your life?" Tory leaned forward, resting her arms on the table. She seemed to be trying to read his mind by memorizing his expression.

"A plan? Nothing concrete," he managed after a moment's consideration, distracted by Tory's sudden avid interest. She seemed to be waiting for his answer with an unnatural expectancy. "I was always going to work for the family firm. I was still in college when my father died, and Preston was out of the country. My grandfather called me into his office and explained what he expected from his only grandson, especially since Preston hadn't showed any inclination toward starting a family."

"It's a little cut-and-dried," Tory murmured. She lowered her eyelashes, cloaking her expression. She didn't look up again, more interested in her fingertip tracing the rim of her coffee cup. "Did he pick out a suitable bride for you, too?"

"Not old L.W. He didn't have much time for women, except as decorations. Herrington men tend to marry late and select women who are an asset to the firm." He smiled as he remembered Preston's sudden marriage six years ago, close to his fiftieth birthday, and to everyone's astonishment. Babs's dowry consisted of her camera and photographs. "My father was the exception, but I've haven't given it much thought. Maybe we should have put that on my questionnaire."

He knew he said something wrong as soon as the words were out of his mouth. Tory stiffened, then abruptly got to her feet.

"What about you? Is there a master plan for Tory Planchet's life?"

"Not really, just building a successful business." *Hopefully I'm better at that than my love life*, she told herself, noting that her hand was shaking as she put her cup and saucer in the sink. "I'm not in any hurry to get married."

What else could she say when she'd fallen in love with a man whose family had a history of marriages of convenience? No wonder he could be so clinical when he talked about having an affair. She'd promised to teach Logan to be more human, but she really wanted to know if he could learn to love. She was undoubtedly setting herself up for more heartache by trying.

"That sounds like a good plan to me," Logan commented, his husky voice much closer than she anticipated. She hadn't heard him get up from the table and cross the room.

She waited to turn away from the sink until he placed his dishes on the counter. She'd known he was close, but not standing directly behind her. The heat from his body reached out to her, tempting her to link her arms around his neck and pull his mouth down to hers. Her mind was at war with her body.

Shaking her head, she knew she was too tired to be dealing with Logan. She'd been assailed by ambiguous emotions all day, trying to analyze and re-analyze her emotions. Tonight on the *Spirit* proved that she couldn't mix her personal and professional life without courting disaster.

Logan's hands framed her face in a warm caress, his thumbs feathering over her cheekbones. She gripped the edge of the counter to keep her hands at her sides. One look into his smoky-blue eyes almost broke her resolve.

"Do I get my reward for rescuing the dessert?" he murmured, searching her face for the answer, waiting for her to respond.

She wet her lips, unable to move away, still trapped by his heated gaze. Dreading and anticipating his kiss as his head lowered, the slam of the back door closing caused her to jerk in reaction.

"Have I interrupted something interesting?" T.L. asked from the kitchen doorway, his voice echoing around the tension filled room. His twinkling eyes took in every detail of the close conjunction of the two occupants. "If I did, I'll just go upstairs quietly, and you can pretend I was never here."

"No one could ever pretend you weren't around, Daddy," Tory stated in exasperation at the interested look on T.L.'s face. Her relief at her father's return was mixed with dread at what he'd say next. Taking the coward's way out, she quickly decided to leave before the situation turned embarrassing.

"I'm glad to see you, but it's been a long day," she announced, walking quickly to the door. Giving T.L. a hasty kiss on the cheek, she waved vaguely in Logan's direction. "Goodnight, gentlemen."

Before either of them could speak, she was out the door. As she ran across the lawn, she wondered if a thirty-year-old woman ever considered running away from home. That might be the only solution to her current problems. She'd leave Abby in charge of the shops, and find a place to hide until Logan went back to Boston. Once he was gone, she could pick up the remnants of her life and pretend that this interlude never happened.

She knew the plan was ridiculous by the time she reached her cottage. A Planchet didn't run away from their problems, no matter how attractive the solution might seem. But being separated from Logan might help. She needed some breathing space. Maybe she would come to her senses without Logan's disturbing presence.

T.L. was back, so she could concentrate on Bill of Fare. After a few days, she could test her resolve, determine if she was in love or simply infatuated. If it was the former, she'd just have to take the rest of Logan's visit one day at a time and hope she survived.

NINE

The sound of a car door slamming reached Logan's sensitive ears as he sat in the gazebo, but he didn't look up. He kept his eyes fixed on the screen of the portable computer he'd purchased the previous day. Even if the new arrival was Tory, it didn't matter. She'd been avoiding him for three days, leaving him at the mercy of her father, just as she had Saturday night in the kitchen.

T.L. hadn't said a word about the scene he interrupted, yet. Logan was still waiting for the other shoe to drop. Just another strange situation that Tory had managed for him. How many men his age were worried about getting lectured by his lover's father? He grimaced at his wishful thinking. Did one night in her arms make them lovers?

"I'm not interrupting anything, am I?"

His fingers skidded over the keyboard and left a trail of garbage on the screen. Tory was standing only a few feet away from him. Taking his time, he saved the file and turned off the computer before he looked at her. He knew it was childish, but she didn't have to have the upper hand all the time. Besides, he was the one who'd played chess, and lost, to T.L. for the past three nights.

"Hello." The greeting was the best he could manage. For the past seventy-two hours he'd only seen her from a distance, and in his dreams. She always seemed to be leaving when he was arriving—whether it was a room, the house, or the property. He'd decided to wait, allowing her a little freedom, even if he was making himself miserable. Why was she seeking his company now?

"Is that your new toy? Trevor said the two of you went to every computer store in town yesterday."

She looked wonderful, and he greedily drank in the sight of her. Her smile went straight to his heart, making him wonder what, or who, caused the excitement that seemed to radiate from her. Although she was leaning against the door frame with her arms crossed, she seemed to have a precarious hold on her nonchalant pose. Her cotton slacks and tailored blouse didn't give a hint as to where she'd been.

"Yes, that's my new toy," he admitted, his smile a little hesitant. He didn't want to break the spell. Tory was here, she was talking to him, and maybe he could tempt his impatience with the situation for at least five minutes. "Preston called yesterday for a progress report on my articles. He wants the first one by next week, so I charged this little beauty to the company."

"How is he?"

Logan knew by her softened tone that she knew about his uncle's illness. He'd learned more about T.L. and Preston's relationship over the past few days, so he wasn't surprised. It was strange to talk to someone about Preston's illness. No one at home discussed it by Preston's order. "He's getting by, one day at a time. Of course, I only have his word for it. I wrote a long letter to Babs earlier this week to get the facts."

Tory nodded and seemed to understand his reticence, her eyes telegraphing her sympathy for a man they both loved. "You mentioned Babs the other night. I have to confess I had an interesting discussion with Abby before the Ferguson party."

"How interesting?" he prompted. He was intrigued by the sudden flush on her cheeks. What could Abby have said to embarrass Tory?

"It seems it isn't Abby who became an idiot after marrying Gary, but the other way around."

"Pardon?" Somehow the conversation had taken a left turn without him realizing it. But with Tory he'd almost come to expect it. He looked forward to her unstructured thought patterns.

"It seems Gary was feeling a little, er, possessive about his new wife, and wanted to make sure that she didn't miss being single." Tory shrugged, pulling a face that made Logan want to jump out of his chair and kiss her. He usually felt that way, and it always got him in trouble, so he stayed safely in his chair.

"I can understand that. A new relationship is like skating on thin ice and every once in a while someone throws you an anvil to hold." Logan decided icy water wouldn't be a bad idea as Tory's laughter sent a shaft of desire through him. Whatever was bothering her on Saturday had disappeared. Unfortunately, he seemed to have caught her melancholy mood. Why else would he sit around for three days, daydreaming about Tory, and still be acting like a love-sick fool when she was only a few feet away?

"Was that what you came to tell me?" he shot out without trying to mask his impatience.

"What? Uh, no." Tory didn't seem to be following the conversation any better than he was. "I was supposed to tell you about the organizer's meeting tonight at Curtiss's house. They'll be going over the last minute arrangements for the rally on Saturday. We thought you might be interested, sort of a behind-the-scenes approach."

"Giving me more of the total rally experience again?" he asked dryly, unable to resist. The question had an intriguing result, Tory blushed again.

Logan decided he needed a closer look at this phenomenon and stood up. Did he make her nervous? Why else would she look so startled? He forced himself to walk very slowly across the wooden flooring.

"Now, Logan, the ride with Tod was harmless. You probably got some good material out of it, didn't you?" She stood her ground, but looked as though she was ready to take flight any second.

Remembering his determination to be more cautious, he stopped with only a foot of space between them. Casually, he leaned his hip against the railing and raised his hand to grasp the door frame, just inches from Tory's shoulder. His eyes were level with her widened gaze, and she couldn't seem to look away. "There's a lot more material I'd like to explore on the subject. What do you have planned for me during the Arkansas Traveler?"

Logan was forced to repress his smile of satisfaction as Tory took a deep swallow and blinked rapidly in answer. She was responding to the husky innuendo in his voice, not to his words. She could claim she was only interested in friendship, but he was sure she had a vivid memory of their night together. His Tory wasn't doing a very good job of hiding her passionate nature.

"I don't have anything planned for you this time. You'll be going around the control crews with Trevor," she managed a little breathlessly. "I'll be handling the rest of the press and visitors."

"Giving up?" he challenged, letting his fingers

accidently brush against her shoulder. Something flashed in Tory's magnificent eyes, just as he had hoped.

"Certainly not," she shot back immediately, then realized what she'd done. The look she gave him would have burned a lesser man to a crisp. "T.L. is back in town, and I have a business to get off the ground. The shop at Park Plaza is going to be ready to open on Monday."

"Need an extra waiter? I'm told that I'm rather good," he continued. Her show of fire was exactly what he wanted. Maybe he'd been trying the wrong tactics all along. Give the lady just enough to worry about, wondering when, or if, he was going to pounce. He allowed himself a slight smile as he remembered his own words on the way back from Oklahoma. *I'll try to play the little gentleman, but don't be surprised if I suddenly make a grab for you.* It might lack finesse, but it seemed to worry his lady love.

"Beginner's luck, Logan. Bodine was the only one to give you a tip."

"He only gave me money. There are other, more pleasant ways to say thank you. And I still haven't thanked you for my lessons in how to be southern." He leaned forward with no more intent than to see Tory's reaction. It was very satisfactory.

She turned on her heels and started across the lawn, not quite running, but in full retreat. When she reached the driveway, she swung around with her hands on her hips. "You apparently need a better instructor. Maybe Trevor can give you a few pointers when he takes you to Curtiss's. Be ready at six-thirty."

Tory marched across the yard and stomped up the steps, trying to drown out the sound of Logan's laughter. Damn the man, she railed at herself, barely keeping from slamming the back door. She thought it would be safe to face him in broad daylight, but no.

She'd arrived ready to share her news about the opening. In her euphoria, she'd forgotten that Logan was dangerous. After avoiding him for seventy-two hours, she thought she had everything in control again. A few minutes in his company had turned her into a blithering fool, as usual.

Maybe she wasn't in love with him after all. It was maybe just a case of temporary insanity. Well, she wouldn't have to worry about her mental state much longer. After Saturday, she'd be finished with her rally duties and buried in the opening of her shop. During the day she'd be too busy to see Logan, and at night she'd be too exhausted to dream about him.

So, why wasn't she ecstatic about the plan?

"You're right, you shouldn't wear hats."

Logan's hand went to the cap on his head at Tory's teasing words from behind him. *This is just what I need*, he grumbled to himself, wondering how she'd appeared out of thin air. *I'm hot, dusty, and stranded in the middle of a forest all day. Then she decides to talk to me for the first time in two days.* The road rally was spread out over acres of the national forest near Lake Winona, a wilderness only a half hour from Little Rock.

He spread his arms out to give her a better view. Two people could play this war of nerves, but he was going to win eventually. "I was told that if I was going to work on a control crew that I had to wear an official cap and T-shirt. Tod Blaylock's daredevil driving is beginning to look like heaven."

"How did you get drafted?" She was having a hard time hiding her smile. She stood with her thumbs looped in the waist band of her hiking shorts, rocking back and forth on the soles of her track shoes. The blue and red Arkansas

Traveler T-shirt snugly fit her neat waist and breasts, causing Logan's mouth to go dry.

"Trevor came up short on personnel," he started to explain, before a shout from down the dirt road stopped his study of her legs. As he turned in the direction of the finish line, he could hear the unmistakable sound of a car engine. A Corvette came into view at the top of the rise a half mile away, the last turn before the finish line of the stage. "Looks like we're going back to work. Ready, Greg."

The teenager standing a few feet away held up his stop watch, but kept his eyes trained on the flag man standing at the finish line further down the track. Logan raised his clipboard as the Corvette neared the flag man. The flag went down, and Greg called out the time for Logan to record on a row of stickers in front of him. When the low-slung sports car skidded to a stop in front of him, he pealed off the sticker and handed it to the co-driver through the opening in the passenger window.

"You handle this like a professional."

Logan only had time to give Tory a quick look before another shout went up from the flag man. A jeep and a Volkswagon were approaching the finish line. He didn't want to admit that his pulse was racing at double time and his palms were sweating.

Trevor had thrown him into this job with very little explanation. When they'd arrived at the timing control for this stage, only one of the scheduled crew had shown up and at least two people were needed. Logan had been drafted a half hour before they'd run the heat to give the cars their starting times. Now, they were running the second daylight stage with the cars running the same route in the opposite direction. If he'd understood correctly, they'd be doing another stage after dark.

He heard Tory talking to someone behind him, but

was occupied with the cars that seemed to be arriving in a pack. A succession of cars went by in a cloud of dust until only two of the twenty stickers remained on his clipboard. He called out the car numbers to Tom Dantry, the radio operator, sitting under the trees across the road. Subconsciously, he registered that Tory was talking to Tom's wife, Alice. A few minutes later Tom relayed the message that one car was out of the rally, but nothing was reported on the other car yet.

"Hey, Boston, you're doing just fine," Trevor called from behind him. The other man was walking up the incline from the main road, apparently parking further down the road to keep clear of the racers.

Logan gave him a succinct evaluation of his duties as Trevor stopped beside him. "No wonder you have trouble getting people to do this. It's a half hour of high tension, and hours of waiting around in between doing nothing."

"Why do you think I'm on the administrative team? I used to go nuts out here. It could be worse. I've done this in the rain and in twenty-degree weather," the other man returned, his grin widening. He checked his watch and frowned. "The slow sweep should be through in about ten minutes, and hopefully, we'll find out what's happened to our missing car. Who is it?"

Logan checked his clipboard. "Three."

"Uh-oh, that's Walt and Midge. If they're out of the race for good, we're going to hear some colorful language. Midge has been in rare form today."

"I know," Logan stated, curling his mouth to the side as he remembered the redhead from earlier in the day. "She was really laying into Greg when we were starting them. He wasn't doing anything fast enough for her, and they almost started ahead of their time, except Billy had the flag on the front of the car to keep them the full two minutes."

"That's our Midge, a real sweetie. She'll do everything she can to shave a few seconds off their time."

The words were barely out of Trevor's mouth before a shout went up from Billy at the finish line. Nesbitt's gray Mazda was cresting the last rise of the course, and it was clear they were having trouble from the black smoke coming from the back of the car. They were closely followed by the pick-up truck driving slow sweep. Both vehicles were driving about twenty miles an hour.

"Looks like they refused a tow from the slow sweep," Tory commented as she joined the two men a few minutes later. "Since this is the last stage before the dinner break, they might have time to get their repairs done before the night stage."

No one had a chance to reply as the Mazda stopped next to Logan. He peeled off the sticker and handed it to Midge who was glaring at the trio. Tory handed her a plastic cup of water, but the other woman carelessly waved it away, spilling half the contents onto the dirt road. The redhead was still staring at Logan.

"Now I remember you," she snapped, her venomous glare singled out Logan as if she hadn't spoken to him a number of times the previous night. "I'm going to report your crew for holding us up earlier. Don't think you'll get off easy because you're sleeping with the rally master's sister either."

Walt put the car into gear and slowly pulled away, leaving a silent group behind. Logan's glance immediately went to Tory, but she was busy digging a stone out of the dirt with the toe of her shoe. When he looked over at Trevor, the man's eyes were narrowed in an assessing look that went from head to toe.

"Well, I've got to round up some media folks for dinner, so I'll see ya'll later," Tory announced, trotting over to her car before either man could speak.

Reluctantly, Logan glanced at Trevor. The other man was watching him, his expression uncharacteristically malevolent.

"It's amazing what you learn during a rally weekend," he began dryly. Logan let out the breath he'd been unconsciously holding in his burning lungs, wishing he'd sink slowly into the ground. "I need to check in at the service stop, but I think I can be back here in a hour so we can have dinner." He waited for an answer, then nodded when Logan remained mute. "Maybe you'd like to go for a little ride, so we can talk about this in private. You've got a couple hours to *kill*."

Logan couldn't keep from wincing slightly at the emphasis on the last word. Although he'd been waiting the last five days for T.L. to lower the boom, he was totally unprepared to deal with Tory's irate brother. Worst of all, he knew he was blushing for the first time in over a decade, or more. Lost in his own thoughts, he didn't realize that Trevor was gone without another word.

The next hour seemed endless. Logan paced the clearing where the crew had setup camp for the day. He made idle conversation with Tom and Alice while Billy and Greg played catch. He knew his minutes were numbered when Alice began unpacking a picnic basket from the back of the station wagon. Almost on cue the sound of an engine alerted him to a new arrival coming from the main road.

When the black 4 x 4 pulled into the clearing, Logan could barely suppress his groan of despair. It was going to be worse than he anticipated. Trevor wasn't alone. He'd brought Curtiss back with him. There would be two irate brothers to deal with. After a quick word to Tom, he reluctantly walked toward the two men. Curtiss got out, waving Logan ahead of him into the vehicle.

No one spoke as Trevor backed out of the clearing and headed for the main road that traversed the lake. Sandwiched between the Planchet brothers, Logan knew what a condemned man felt like. He figured he didn't have anything to lose, but was amazed his voice was level. "I suppose I should be grateful you haven't had time to call in your truck driver friends."

"She told you about that, did she?" Trevor didn't take his eyes off the road, driving at a speed that would have disqualified any of the rally participants between stages. "I'm surprised. She thinks she can take care of herself, especially after she got rid of her fiancé, with a little help from a pitcher of beer."

"Her fiancé?" Logan growled the two words, forgetting about making a defense against Midge's statement. A tight knot settled in the pit of his stomach at the news that Tory had been engaged to another man. He wanted to take the unknown man by the scruff of his neck and throw him out of Tory's life, although she'd already apparently sent him on his way.

"You don't know about old Reed?" Curtiss asked, exchanging a surprised look with his brother.

"No," Logan spat out the word. He didn't think they needed to look so pleased about the news. Then he wondered what the Planchets intended when Trevor pulled off the road onto a dirt track. They drove on for about a mile, stopping near a stone bridge that arched over a stream that undoubtedly fed the nearby lake. Were they planning to hide his battered body here in this bucolic hideaway?

Neither Trevor nor Curtiss said a word. They climbed out of the vehicle, walked to the back, and opened the door. Logan's view was restricted to the rear view mirror. They were discussing something and pointing behind the back seat. Trevor lifted something heavy, then looked up to meet Logan's gaze in the mirror. He seemed surprised that the other man hadn't moved.

"You do want to eat dinner, don't you?" he asked as he handed the green-and-white cooler to his brother and tucked a blanket under his arm. "We've got another eight hours or so out here, so you'd better eat something."

"I'm not sure I have any appetite," Logan answered, but got out of the car anyway. By the time he joined the men at the edge of the stream, a picnic had been spread out on the flat rocks that flanked the water. Absently, he wondered if Tory had prepared the meal of cold chicken, marinated raw vegetables, and crusty rolls. "Exactly what happened to this Reed person?"

"Why do you want to know?" The assessing gleam was back in Trevor's eyes—eyes that were so similar to his sister's. He bit into a drumstick, but never took his gaze off Logan.

"Damn it, I love Tory." The words came out of nowhere, echoing off the bluffs on the opposite side of the stream, and inside Logan's brain. He knew his expression probably matched Curtiss's and Trevor's opened-mouth astonishment. Although he hadn't realized his own feelings until that moment, Logan knew he was speaking the truth. There wasn't another woman in the world like Tory Planchet, and she belonged to him.

"Hell, I was going to ask what your intentions were and you spoiled my big speech," Trevor complained, doing his best to look put out by Logan's bald announcement. He wiped his fingers on a paper napkin, frowning as he finished the task.

"That certainly put a damper on our plan. We rehearsed a great speech on the way over to pick you up. I was going to be the nice brother and Trevor was going to play the heavy, like good-cop-bad-cop," Curtiss put in, then anxiously looked up at Logan through the fringe of his bangs. "You *are* serious, aren't you?"

"I'm afraid so," Logan answered, looking from one man to the other. He didn't blame them for being skeptical.

"You're a brave man. My sister is the most independent woman I know. There are two things that she doesn't have any patience with, bossy men and Yankees." Trevor shrugged philosophically and shared a commiserating look with his brother. "You're batting zero to two in this ball game, Boston."

"You don't think I have a snowball's chance of marrying your sister, then?"

"Let's say I won't put any money on you to win. Marriage doesn't seem to be in her game plan," Trevor continued, but not letting the discussion interfere with his dinner. Curtiss seemed content to let his older brother hold center stage, simply nodding his agreement and helping himself to another piece of chicken. "Bill of Fare has been her first priority since she gave Reed the old heave-ho six years ago. Besides, the Planchet track record hasn't been very good."

"You've lost me. What's wrong with Planchet marriages? You and Sanders seem to be handling marriage fairly well." Logan made a grab for the chicken before the other two cleaned the plate. His appetite had suddenly returned with the news that there weren't any serious contenders in Tory's life and hadn't been for six years.

"It's T.L. He's only had one successful marriage out of three. Sander's mother lasted about five years," Curtiss explained hesitantly. "If Tory and Trevor's mother hadn't been killed in a car accident, I doubt if I'd have come along. T.L. only married my mother because he was lonely after Miriam died. My mother walked out when I was three.''

"Personally, I've always found it encouraging that his one success was with Mother, but I'm not sure if Tory feels the same way." Trevor handed Logan a soft drink before opening his own and taking a swig from the can. "Tory was at an impressionable age when Curtiss's mother hit the road. Angela had been a poor substitute for us and T.L. She knew Daddy was still grieving, and they had some dandy screaming matches.''

"You might be right," Logan said thoughtfully. Tory's attitude toward marriage wasn't exactly encouraging. Could Trevor be right? Was she avoiding marriage because of her childhood memories? It seemed pretty farfetched to him.

"As I said, you're a brave man. Trying to get a commitment out of a bossy, stubborn woman like my sister is a monumental task." Trevor stretched out and propped himself up with his elbows. Contemplating the beginning traces of the sunset above the trees, he continued, "Don't get me wrong. I love my sister. Unfortunately, she's not a restful woman. I prefer them a little more malleable and soft-spoken.''

"That's the truth. Leeanne is much easier to live with," Curtiss stated. "Someone like Tory would drive me crazy in about a week.''

"That's part of her charm. She doesn't hold back,'' *even when she makes love*, he finished to himself, remembering her wholehearted lovemaking that night in Oklahoma. "You know, you're both taking this very well. What happened to all that brotherly advice when you kept fiddling with your steak knife, Trevor?''

"I like you, and I think my sister is beginning to like you a little too much for her peace of mind. She's letting this North/South nonsense cloud her judgment.''

"What do I do, change my birth certificate?"

"You might try being a little more southern," Trevor decided, after a moment's concentrated effort. He looked extremely proud of his inspiration. "I think she's just using this Yankee nonsense as a smoke screen. She's never been that rabid about the subject until you came along. That just proves you're getting under her skin."

"Women like all that attention if you hold doors open, pull out their chairs, and that stuff. I did that before Leeanne and I got married. Must have spent a fortune on flowers before I proposed, too."

"All I have to do is get Tory to stand still long enough." Logan didn't bother to explain that the southern strategy had been tried without great success. He hoped Trevor was right, however, about Tory using their regional differences as a defense mechanism.

"Well, I know how you can get her attention for about a half hour," Trevor volunteered. He began gathering up the remnants of their meal as he spoke. "If Curtiss and I play it right, you'll be riding back to Little Rock with her after the rally."

"Gentlemen, you'll be my friends for life."

"Don't make any rash promises until after you talk to Tory," he returned, giving him a look of masculine understanding. He'd been on the losing side of an argument with his sister once too often. "And whatever you do, don't tell Tory we had this little talk."

Logan nodded, but was silent on the way back to the control station, plotting how to handle the ride back to Little Rock. He had to convince Tory he was the man for her, the man who would have a permanent place in her life. Why hadn't he realized he was in love sooner? He felt like a fool for not seeing the signs before this.

SOUTHERN HOSPITALITY / 177

He'd known from the minute that he met her at the airport that Tory was different, but simply put it down to physical attraction. Everything she did fascinated him. He was frustrated every moment they were apart.

How did he convince a woman who wouldn't have an affair that he loved her? *Excuse me, Tory, what I thought was simple lust turned out to be love*. Logan shook his head in disgust. He'd have to do much better than that, but what? He hadn't done anything right since the moment he met her.

Suddenly, he wondered how the Herrington family had managed to survive over the last few hundred years. He'd been taught not to be overly emotional, to always appear calm and controlled in any circumstance. The Puritan strain ran deep. How did the Pilgrims manage to marry and produce children? Did they have secret hand signals or something to keep from making total idiots of themselves when they fell in love?

When the Planchet brothers dropped him off, he wondered how they were going maneuver Tory in driving him back to the city. But he decided he had enough problems of his own. They'd known her long enough to manage something, and he had to figure out how to overcome two hundred years of repression.

Tory slammed the door of her car. She'd left the motor running, ready to get her duty over as soon as possible. Leaning against the front fender, she glared at the group working to clean up the control site. Logan had his back to her as he kicked dirt over the last embers of the fire. She was sure he knew she was there and why. Neither Curtiss nor Trevor were very good actors. They'd been too astonished over forgetting to arrange a ride for Logan. Rather than let the painful performance continue, she volunteered, almost changing her mind when she saw the smug look that passed between her brothers.

What was going on here? After Midge's little bombshell, her brothers conspiring with Logan certainly wasn't what she expected. Then again, her life had been full of surprises lately. She hadn't anticipated falling in love with Logan, either.

"Hey, Logan, looks like you won't have to hitchhike back to Little Rock after all," Tom Dantry called from where he was loading folding chairs into the back of his station wagon. He gave Tory a friendly wave before going back to work.

She waited with her arms crossed over her breasts, trying to pretend her heart was not in overdrive at the sight of his lean figure walking toward her. His long, jean encased legs ate up the ground between them much too quickly for her peace of mind. She'd had a long day and wasn't ready for another confrontation, either mental or physical.

What was it about his expression that was different? Maybe it was the angle of her headlights, or was she imagining things after a long day? When he reached the front of the car, she jerked her head toward the passenger seat. Without bothering to see if he complied, she turned and got into the driver's seat.

Logan joined her before she moved the gearshift into drive. She honked in farewell to the Dantrys, then executed a sweeping turn to head for the main road. At this hour of the night, she estimated she might reach Little Rock in about twenty minutes.

Logan was slumped down in his seat, not saying a word. Just as Tory began to speculate whether he'd fallen asleep, he rolled his head along the back of the seat to stare at her. She felt more than saw the flash of his smile in the dim interior of the car.

"You know I could get used to this," he murmured. The softly-spoken words seemed to feather across the back of her neck before shivering down her spine.

"Get used to what?" she was forced to ask when he let the comment hang in the air. Her fingers tightened on the steering wheel as she willed herself to ignore a growing sense of intimacy in the close confines of the car.

"I could get used to your chauffeuring me around from place to place," he returned quietly, amusement underlying his words.

"Isn't that a little chauvinistic?" Why was she whispering? If she just spoke in a normal tone, it would dispel the illusion they were the only two people in the world. The deserted road didn't help matters. There wasn't another car in sight along the highway, which wasn't unexpected after midnight.

"Tell me about Reed, Tory."

She was going to break the steering wheel in two, she was sure of it, gripping it even tighter. Her brothers had to have told him about Reed. Was that what was responsible for the difference she'd sensed in him earlier?

"You'd better slow down a little," Logan suggested without seeming too upset by the speed they were traveling. "I don't think you want to get a ticket or damage your new car."

"It's a rental. I never take one of our cars to a rally, too much gravel and dirt," she commented, but lowered her speed to fifty-five. She hadn't realized that she'd accelerated to twenty miles over the speed limit. It must have been his question about Reed.

"You were going to tell me about Reed."

Thankfully, the highway was a fairly straight road that led directly into the city. She didn't have to concentrate on her steering too much. "Was I?"

"Was it that bad?"

"No one likes to admit to being stupid. I met him when I was in college. We got engaged and were apart for a year," Tory stated the facts in a rapid rush of words. She wanted to get this over with as quickly as possible, although she wasn't sure she wanted to know where the conversation was leading. "I came back from Paris and discovered that we had nothing in common. Reed wanted me to play the brainless woman to his lord and master."

"Not a very bright man," Logan commented, the undercurrent of amusement returning.

"No, and he didn't have much of a sense of humor either. He made one condescending remark too many about my intelligence at dinner one night. I'm afraid I let my temper get out of hand and poured a pitcher of beer over him."

"How much beer was there?"

"It was about half full."

"I don't drink beer, Tory."

"It's just as well. I never repeat myself, even when I'm angry."

"Don't confuse me with your fiancé either. I think you're an intelligent, beautiful woman." His words were soft and dangerous. He was making love to her without even touching her. "We're going to make love again, Tory Planchet. We're good together, too good to let you deny what's between us. It might take some time to convince you, but I will."

She didn't know what to say. His tone was gentle, almost caressing, making her start to melt inside, until she recognized the underlying demand. Why did men feel this arrogant need to assert themselves? Just because she'd fallen in love with him, didn't mean Logan could tell her what to do.

Slowing the car, she decided to give Logan her opinion of the situation. Just as she was about to pull off the road, she realized there was a change in the atmosphere. The tension between them had dissipated somehow. She turned to look at Logan and discovered the reason. He was asleep.

Her immediate reaction was to wake him up and tell him once and for all that she wasn't going to have an affair with him. She reconsidered a minute later. Let him sleep and give her some peace. A smile curved her lips by the time she reached the city limits. Could she really leave him sleeping in the car when she got back to the house? That might make him think twice about making smug, masculine demands.

TEN

Logan looked at his watch for the sixth or seventh time in the last ten minutes. Muttering under his breath, he began pacing the length of Tory's living room again. Where was she? It was almost seven o'clock. She couldn't still be at the shop. He gave vent to his frustration with a few choice words.

The day had been a total disaster as far as he was concerned—from the moment he woke up around eleven o'clock. He hated sleeping late, especially when it meant he'd missed catching Tory before she'd gone out. His mood wasn't improved by only remembering bits and pieces of the ride home the previous night. The warmth of the car was relaxing after the hours spent outdoors had taken their toll, and he'd fallen asleep. What a way to impress the woman he loved.

Was Tory being elusive because of something he'd said during the ride? He didn't remember much after asking about her fiancé, except her nudging him awake and shuffling up to bed. He'd been one step behind her all day, just missing her at the shop and returning to the house to discover she'd gone out again. Finally, he decided to stay in one place until she came home. Her cottage was the ideal place, if she ever came home.

Stalking into the dining alcove, he looked over the table once more. Everything was in place—china, silver, peach-colored candles, and the matching dozen roses in the center of the table. Maybe he should check on dinner again as well, although there wasn't much he could do until Tory made an appearance. Everything was ready to put in the oven, once the guest of honor arrived. The sound of footsteps approaching the front door held him in place. Suddenly he wondered if he was doing the right thing, but it was too late with Tory walking in.

"What are you doing here?" she challenged, startled to find him standing in the doorway between the living room and the dining area.

"I figured you had a rough day today, so I'm putting all that good, courteous southern training to use," he explained. Now that the waiting was over his confidence returned, allowing him to walk toward her with a slight swagger. From her expression, he couldn't have done anything too incredibly stupid last night. "Let me take your jacket, then you sit down and put your feet up."

She followed his instructions, but watched his every move. He smiled at her wary look when he returned from hanging her jacket in the hallway. She sat perched on the edge of the couch with her hands folded primly in her lap.

"That isn't any way to relax," he chided, walking to the armoire that concealed her television and stereo. Opening the door he flipped on the radio to the classical station he'd found earlier. "You look like one of those poker-stiff portraits of my ancestors that Mother insists on displaying at home. Sit back and put your feet up."

"Logan, what's going on?" she finally protested

after he'd plumped the tasseled throw pillows and moved the needlepoint ottoman close to the couch. When he reached for her feet, she jerked away, tucking them safely under her. "Cut that out, and give me an explanation."

Trying to look crestfallen at her peremptory order, he sat on the ottoman. "Arnette told me you were out all day getting your shop ready for tomorrow's opening. Being a southerner in training, I had an inspiration. You shouldn't have to do a thing for yourself tonight, so you'll be nice and relaxed tomorrow morning."

She tilted her head to the side and nibbled her lower lip. Suspicion lurked in the back of her eyes, but after a minute a tentative smile appeared. "Can I go change my clothes by myself? Please? I've been in the same outfit all day, hauling equipment, yelling at the staff, and cooking."

"No problem. Your wish is my command," he said easily, although he was tempted to offer to help her change. But he knew better than to press his luck. So far, so good. He was going to be as impersonal as his mother's butler, at least for a while. "I'll go pour you a glass of wine while you change."

An hour later Tory dropped onto the couch with a sigh of contentment. "Logan, I think you might just have earned your southern diploma tonight. Dinner was wonderful." Propping her slippered feet on the ottoman, she draped the skirt of her silk caftan over her legs and sat back among the pillows. "There was only a minor problem, but I think I can overlook it this one time."

"A problem? Did I forget something?" He was puzzled, unable to think of anything he'd missed as he knelt to light the fire. Once the flames took hold, he served her a snifter of cognac with a flourish and settled himself on the floor in front of the couch at Tory's feet.

"Nothing too serious. If you really want to impress me, don't serve me food from one of my major competitors." Her reprimand was softened by a chuckle. "Or at least hide the evidence better."

"Guess I should have thrown out the boxes sooner," he agreed, smiling ruefully over his shoulder. Silently he wondered how much longer he could maintain the pose of a lapdog. Ironically, Curtiss's and Trevor's advice yesterday didn't seem too off the mark. Tory seemed to be responding to the gentlemanly approach. Why hadn't any of his efforts worked until tonight? Maybe Trevor was right as well about Tory exaggerating her dislike of northerners.

"Don't I get some points for working on a tight schedule? Besides, your shops aren't open yet, so I had to play it by ear."

"You have a point."

With the matter settled, Logan didn't bother to answer. The soft strains of Chopin filled the room as they sat in amicable silence. Logan allowed his mind to wander into a fantasy world. This was how it would be if he could persuade Tory to marry him. They'd sit at home, discussing what they'd done during the day. The children would be asleep, letting their parents have some quality time to themselves.

"Logan, did you happen to see any large pods out in the woods yesterday?"

"What?" Tory's question jarred him out of his pleasant daydream just as he was about to carry his wife to bed. "Pods?"

"Didn't you ever see *Invasion of the Body Snatchers*?"

Giving her a curious look, he tried to think of the plot to the movie. Concentrating was hard with Tory so close, and so inviting. Her dark hair was loose around her shoulders, her maple-colored eyes slumberous and sparkling with suppressed laughter. The silk of her caftan lovingly outlined her small breasts, the zipper leading from the V-neck inviting him to explore. The invitation of her smile had his lower body tightening in response.

"Give up?" she teased, running her finger around the rim of her glass. Her smile widened when he nodded. "People who slept near the pods changed personalities. I thought you might have come across some during the rally."

He stared at her, knowing the moment had arrived to give up his charade. Her smile wavered slightly as he reached for her glass. He placed it on the marble top of the coffee table along with his, then hoisted himself up on the couch next to Tory. This was what he'd wanted to do all night.

"You have to make up your mind, sweetheart. Which man do you want?" He spoke softly, draping his arm along the back of the couch. Moving slowly, he gently moved her hair back behind her ear, tracing the line of her jaw with the movement. "Do you want tonight's polite eunuch, or this man?"

As his mouth closed over hers, Tory's last thought was, *This man.* She allowed herself the magic of one kiss. One kiss couldn't be so dangerous. They were both reasonable adults who could control their emotions. Then Logan gently coaxed her lips apart with the tip of his tongue.

She knew she should resist, but the sensations that he evoked were too tempting. It was just one kiss. Boldly she reached up to thread her fingers through his thick golden-brown hair. When he groaned deep in his throat, she dared to challenge his intimate invasion of her mouth. She began a passionate duel that had her sinking further into the world of pure sensation.

To her surprise, Logan broke the contact of their lips. But she wasn't disappointed. His lips trailed over her cheek to explore the soft skin below her ear. Murmuring her approval, she leaned closer to the warmth of his hard body. She stroked the tense muscles of his back, wishing his shirt wasn't covering the taut skin beneath.

"Now, isn't that better than having some genderless fool hanging around?" he whispered, his warm breath setting off a thousand tiny sparks within her.

For a moment, she couldn't breathe. His tongue was tracing the outline of her ear. "Are you trying to seduce me?"

Logan pulled back. His eyes were a deep, stormy gray as they searched her face. She stroked the side of his face, the smooth skin telling her he'd shaved recently. The evidence of his preparation didn't alarm her.

He turned slightly, his lips feathering over her palm before the tip of his tongue repeated the caress. "Would it be so terrible if I was?"

She had trouble remembering what they were talking about. Her mind seemed to be functioning in slow motion, but a small, inner voice warned her to be cautious. "Tonight I'm not sure."

"Consider it a reward for a man going on a journey." His finger skimmed over her jaw to trace the line of her throat to her collarbone. From there, he continued to explore new territory with the back of his fingers, settling in the shadowed valley of her cleavage.

"You're going away?" Her voice sounded distant to her ears, but talking wasn't high on her list of priorities at the moment. She was much more interested in the play of his clever fingers that were toying with the pull of her zipper.

"Yes, I'm going to Paris, Texas, tomorrow. There's a rally next weekend, so I'm going to spend some time scouting out the countryside."

The thought of him going away made the decision for

Tory. She didn't consider the contradiction of avoiding him for the past week while he was near at hand. Tonight would be the last time she would have any intimate contact with the man she'd inexplicably come to love in such a short amount of time. She wouldn't deny herself the pleasure of one last night in his arms. It would be her farewell to something that couldn't be, and much better to make a clear break now, instead of waiting until he returned to Boston.

She played with the button at the top of his shirt, dipping her fingers under the collar of his shirt to explore his warm skin and feeling the steady beat of his heart. She smiled at the sudden intake of his breath as she exerted pressure and his button slipped through the button hole.

"Are you going to make me do all the work?" She thrust out her lower lip. Watching him from the screen of her eyelashes, she dared him to continue his sensual assault.

She wasn't prepared for Logan's reaction. He jumped to his feet, scooping her up into his arms before she knew what was happening. Her arms looped around his neck in a tight grip as she wondered if they'd make it to the bedroom. Logan didn't falter. Guided by the dim light of the hall, he set her back on her feet next to the bed.

Tory wasn't sure what to do. She nervously twisted her hands together as Logan reached over to turn on the milk-glass lamp on the nightstand. Then he turned back to her, his hand reaching for her zipper. He hesitated for a moment. There was a questioning look on his face, giving him a vulnerability that was incongruous with his usual self-assurance.

Any doubts she had were allayed as she recognized his sudden defenselessness. She made quick work of the buttons down the front of his shirt, pulling it free of his waistband and opening the material to expose his chest. Closing her eyes for a moment, she savored the hair roughed texture against her palms, moving her hands back to his shoulders before burrowing beneath the material to slip it off his body.

Logan's body was tense under her exploration. His eyes were hooded, but didn't hide the lambent gray-blue fire as he slowly pulled on the zipper of her caftan. She tried to repress the slight shiver of excitement as he bared her body to his hungry gaze. Suddenly the soft material was in a pool at her feet, leaving her cloaked only in a scrap of silk at her hips. He didn't touch her, seeming satisfied to study her graceful figure in the soft light.

"No, let me," he whispered when she started to step out of her slippers. His hands closed over her shoulders, holding her in place as his eyes ran over her. He began at her rounded breasts, then slowly moved to the indentation of her waist, coming to rest on the thrust of her hips. His lips willingly followed the same path as he kissed his way down her body until he was on his knees before her. His compelling hands feathered down the length of her legs until they met at the heel of one slipper.

Tory closed her eyes against the exquisite delight. Logan removed each slipper, taking his time. Burying his face in the slight swell of her stomach, his hands moved upward to massage her firm buttocks, holding her in place. She moaned in response to the heat building in her as his lips traveled over the last barrier that veiled her from his sight.

She gazed in fascination at the top of his tousled head against her skin. Any minute she thought she'd explode from the intoxication that was building inside her. She'd made the right decision. This would be a memory she'd have for the rest of her life, no matter what happened. Tangling her fingers in his golden-brown hair, she tilted his face upward. His stormy eyes reflected her own excitement.

He rose to his feet and cupped her face gently in his hands, hands that were trembling slightly. "I can't wait much longer. I've been thinking and hoping for this since that incredible night in Oklahoma."

"Have you?" She didn't recognize her own voice, husky with passion as his unsteady fingers removed her panties. She tried again when he pulled her into his arms, her sensitive breasts nestling into the heat of his chest. "Oh, Logan, I need you, too. Don't wait. Next time you can be my gallant gentleman."

"Next time? Oh, love, I hope you're not overestimating my stamina," he answered, triumph in his laugh as he swept her into his arms once more. When he placed her on the bed, he hastily dealt with the rest of his clothes. His hot gaze never leaving her body. "I've dreamed of you like this so many times since I carried you to bed that night. Leaving you alone was one of the hardest things I've ever done."

"You don't have to leave tonight," she promised, opening her arms to take him into her embrace.

They didn't waste time on preliminaries. Both of them were already too impatient for the ultimate joining. His tongue explored her moist lips as he entered her feminine core. She wrapped her legs around his hips wanting to take all of him inside her. Their tentative, slow foreplay was forgotten. He moved over her in a steady rhythm that she gladly met.

She wanted to return every ounce of pleasure he was giving her, share the incredible tension that was growing, flowering inside her. His hands were moving over her, branding her with each touch. When his lips moved to suckle the pebble-hard peaks of her breasts, she cried out. She was spinning out of control and the only thing that would save her was holding on to the man who was taking her closer and closer to the vortex.

Impatiently, she quickened the pace. Her hands grasped his hips. The heated nucleus of her desire seemed to shatter into a thousand pieces of sparkling lights that coursed through every portion of her body. "Logan!"

He captured the sound with a searing kiss, reaching the peak of his gratification. They descended back to reality, his arms wrapped securely around her damp body. Slowly he rolled onto his side without breaking the connection of their bodies as a sweet lethargy settled over them.

Tory nestled her head in the crook of his shoulder, hiding her face against his neck. Her body was still trembling in reaction, her breath shallow. She could feel his rapid heart beat under her hand and couldn't resist the tactile exploration for his chest.

"Tory?"

Pressing her fingers against his lips, she made a shushing sound against the taut column of his throat. She didn't want to spoil the magic of the moment by talking. This was her night to dream. Tomorrow would be the time for talk. Until then, she would express her love with her body, giving Logan a precious memory when she said goodbye.

She sought his lips, trailing kisses as she went. Her reward was Logan's moan of delight. As her body dissolved into his, she felt the rebirth of his desire growing inside her.

Tory climbed down from the truck and stretched her arms over her head to relieve her tired muscles. She'd been working extra hours in the week since Logan had gone to Texas. For the hundredth time she wondered how he reacted to the note she left beside him on the pillow the morning he left.

She'd woken up at dawn and knew she couldn't face him. Leaving him peacefully sleeping, she went to the kitchen. Writing her farewell was the hardest thing she'd ever done. When she'd returned to the bedroom for her clothes, one look at Logan had tempted her to return to bed.

Memories of the night almost overwhelmed her, but she knew there wasn't a future for them. No matter how much he tried to fit her pattern of the ideal mate, it couldn't happen. She valued her independence too much to become involved with a man with Logan's temperament. It was better to say goodbye now when there was less heartache. She'd turned and walked out the door, trying to ignore the tears in her eyes.

Dragging her feet, she went up the back steps to the main house. She didn't want to be alone tonight. Maybe T.L. could distract her from her thoughts of Logan.

"Well, it's about time you got home, young lady," Arnette said as she walked into the kitchen. "You're working yourself into the ground with this new store."

"I had the last interviews for sales staff today. Next week it won't be so bad," Tory prevaricated. Next week wouldn't be any different. Work was the only thing that kept her mind off her personal problems.

"Don't sit down. You march yourself into the front parlor and help your daddy entertain his guest," the older woman ordered. Tory hovered next to the chair she'd pulled out. "I had orders to hold dinner until you arrived, so march."

"I really don't think I'll be good comp—"

"That's an order. Besides, T.L.'s going to need all the help he can get with that one."

"Who is it, Arnette?" Tory was intrigued by her tone of voice. There weren't very many people who got on Arnette's bad side.

"I don't want to ruin the surprise. You need to experience this without any warning."

Knowing she wouldn't get any more information from Arnette, Tory followed her instructions. She could hear T.L.'s voice as she walked down the hall and was surprised to hear a feminine voice respond. A woman? A warning bell went off inside her head. Could T.L. have brought home a woman to introduce to the family? Is that what had Arnette in a snit?

Please tell me I'm wrong, Tory pleaded silently as she stood in the parlor archway. The woman was tall, elegant, and looked as if she were smelling something bad. She sat poker-straight in one of the armchairs. The regal tilt of her head and the sleek, upsweep hairstyle made Tory think of royalty. The inner alarm rang again when the woman turned to regard Tory, but this time she knew her guess was more accurate. Logan must have inherited his eyes from his mother's side of the family.

"Ah, Victoria, there you are," T.L. practically boomed across the room. He was on his feet and walking toward her like a man reaching for a life preserver. "We have a visitor. I was truly amazed when I came home to discover that Logan's mother decided to pay us a visit."

He latched onto Tory's arm, almost as if he was afraid she'd try to escape. Pulling her alongside him, he returned to Mrs. Herrington's side. "Victoria, this is Enid Herrington. Enid, my daughter, Victoria."

"How do you do?" Tory said formally, taking the limp, pale hand that Enid Herrington extended. Things must be pretty bad if T.L. was calling her Victoria.

"Charmed," Enid managed, sounding anything but delighted. "Tyrone has been telling me about your little food business. You keep very unusual hours here in Arkansas."

Tory didn't know how to respond and looked at T.L. for some guidance. No one called her daddy Tyrone.

"Enid doesn't believe in nicknames, Victoria. Isn't that interesting?" T.L. raised his eyebrows and gave her a sickly smile that said, *Do something*!

"It's a shame that Logan is out of town right now," Tory began, wondering how she could ask if he'd been expecting his mother. Or did he know she was coming and leave town on purpose?

"Actually I came on the spur of the moment, something I don't usually do, of course. But I just had to see for myself what Preston had gotten Logan involved in down here." She smoothed her hand over the skirt of her beige suit, which matched her beige hair and beige skin.

"Have you visited Arkansas before?" Tory asked, determined to find something she could talk about to this woman. She sat down on the sofa next to T.L. and was surprised at the strange noises he began to make at her question. He gave a short cough when she gave him an inquiring look.

"No, Victoria, I have never been here," Enid returned, straightening her spine with exaggerated care. "I can't think of any reason I would need to, actually. Once I've taken care of this nonsensical trip of Logan's, I doubt I'll ever come back."

"Dinner."

Arnette's call to dinner cut off the sharp retort Tory was about to deliver. As T.L. made a show of escorting Enid to the dining room, Tory exchanged an understanding look with Arnette. It was possible one of them would kill the woman before her wandering son returned. If she did give into the temptation, Tory was sure Arnette would help her hide the body.

*　　*　　*

"What an interesting piano. Do you play, Victoria?" Enid asked as she walked back into the sitting room after dinner the second night of her visit.

Tory wondered if Enid Herrington had anything in her wardrobe that wasn't beige. Tonight's outfit was a jersey dress that did nothing to improve her coloring. Smiling at the thought, she answered graciously, "No, I don't. Actually, Daddy bought it for the cupids. Isn't that right, Tyrone?"

T.L. choked slightly on his brandy and glared at his daughter. "Yes, Victoria, that's right. No one in the family plays, but I keep it in tune anyway. Arnette told me that Logan's played it a few times during his visit. You've heard him, haven't you, To—Victoria?"

"Yes, he played beautifully." She wasn't going to say another word until she was asked a question. Every minute in Enid Herrington's presence reminded her of the reasons she could never have a lasting relationship with Logan. The woman was the ultimate snob. Logan couldn't forget his years of training, no matter how many southern lessons he passed.

"How nice that he's keeping up with it while he's here," his mother commented. Tory was amazed to see her give a genuine smile for the first time. "I taught him how to play as a child."

"You did?" Tory and T.L. asked in unison.

"Yes, I did. Before my mother decided that I was going to marry Schuyler, I had aspirations of becoming a concert pianist," she explained, her eyes beginning to sparkle at the memory. "Of course, in those days women weren't encouraged to pursue a career. So, I married Schuyler in the biggest wedding that my mother could plan.

"Victoria, you're very lucky that you can work at something you love," Enid commented after taking a sip of Amaretto. "I'd like to see your new shop before I leave, if that's possible."

Tory quickly brought her coffee cup to her lips to keep her mouth from dropping open. Surely Enid Herrington wasn't giving her a compliment. Had she been too hasty in judging her?

"Tomorrow might be a good day. Sunday should be slow. It's hard to tell since we've only been open a week," she found herself saying. "But I don't have any extra catering scheduled, so we won't be doing any extra cooking."

"Thank you, I find catering fascinating. There's so many functions that I organize. What's truly amazing is how creative people can be with food. It must be quite challenging."

"Well, if you ladies are going to discuss food, I think—"

"Now, Daddy, you don't want our guest to think you're rude," Tory said hastily, stopping T.L. as he was halfway out of his chair. She reinforced her words with a fierce look. The woman might be interested in catering, but that didn't mean she wanted to be left alone with her. "I was hoping we could get Enid to play something for us."

"What an excellent idea, just as soon as I refill my glass," he agreed as if he'd simply been standing up to get more brandy, instead of trying to make a getaway.

"Oh, I don't want to impose," Enid said faintly, already flexing her fingers.

"If you taught Logan, we're in for a real treat," Tory returned with genuine enthusiasm.

T.L. gallantly opened the cover of the piano and pulled out the piano stool. Enid didn't seem to need any further encouragement. She took her place, remembering to ask for any requests. When the Planchets demurred, she suggested a little Beethoven. The familiar tune of *Fur Elise* floated across the room. At the last lingering note, Tory and T.L. broke into applause. Even after such a brief piece of music, Enid's talent was evident. They encouraged her to play more.

The next hour sped by as Enid played selections of Bach, Chopin, and Rachmaninoff. As she played her face became flushed, emotion flowing from her fingers. Tory felt as if she was watching a transformation. The colorless woman was changing with each key she touched. Enid seemed to be absorbing the passionate emotion of each composer.

"Madame, we are your slaves for life," T.L. announced when Enid couldn't play another note. He went to her side and executed an elaborate bow.

To Tory's surprise, Enid Herrington giggled. The sound was a little rusty, but it was a giggle. The older woman rose to her feet, then dipped into a deep curtsey as T.L. kissed her hand. Rising to her feet once more, she flashed a broad grin of accomplishment. Logan had inherited his mother's smile as well.

"I haven't done that in years," she exclaimed, brushing back an errant tendril of hair with the back of her hand. "Tyrone, would you happen to have a handkerchief. I seem—"

"At your service, madame," he answered and pulled a snowy piece of linen from his pocket. "As my granddaddy used to say, you're glowing, my dear."

Enid dabbed at her forehead and neck. Giving T.L. a level look that held a definite twinkle, she challenged, "Ladies in the South might glow, but at times ladies from New England perspire. I'd forgotten how taxing playing can be."

Both T.L. and Tory hesitated for a minute, but couldn't contain their laughter when Enid raised one eyebrow.

"You sit down right here, and I'll get you a restorative," T.L. instructed.

"Your father is quite charming, Victoria. I have to admit that I'm enjoying my visit much more than I had anticipated."

"I'm glad, Enid. Thank you for playing for us tonight. Would it be too much to hope for another recital before you leave?"

"I'd love to. Perhaps when Logan returns we can play a Schumann duet that we've performed at a number of functions." Enid continued to smile, making Tory's heart ache at the resemblance to her son. "I hate to admit it, but he's really the better player."

"I'm not a good judge, but I'd say it's a draw," Tory returned, getting to her feet as T.L. returned to the room. "I'll have to excuse myself now. It's been a long day, and I'll have to be back at work again tomorrow. Enid, I'll probably be able to come by about two o'clock tomorrow and we can go over to the shop after lunch."

Once the arrangements were made, Tory escaped. She didn't walk directly back to the cottage, but headed for the gazebo. There was something about the octagonal structure that helped her think. She'd made a number of important decisions there, sitting and watching the silhouette of the Ozark foothills at night.

Enid Herrington's piano playing had her mind in a turmoil. She began to wonder if a lasting relationship with Logan might be possible. Under the right circumstances, both Logan and his mother dropped their Bostonian attitudes. How deep did those attitudes run? Could they just be a facade, a mask to protect them from the outside world?

Perhaps she was being foolish. She missed Logan more than she had anticipated. The week without him had been endless. How was she going to survive the rest of her life? Cutting him out of her life was much more painful than her broken engagement. But then, she realized a long time ago that she hadn't really loved Reed. It had only been a youthful infatuation.

Had she been incredibly stupid to say goodbye to Logan? She had one kernel of hope growing inside her. Logan still might not be willing to take no for an answer. He'd ignored her denials in the past. Would he continue to try and break through her defenses?

Tory got slowly to her feet, letting out a sigh of disappointment. She'd only found more questions tonight. Even if Logan still wanted her, she didn't know for how long. She might have recognized her love, but Logan had only talked of passion and need for a brief period of time.

Patience wasn't one of her best qualities, but she would just have to wait and see what happened. Logan would be back soon. By the end of next week, she would know whether or not her love was returned.

ELEVEN

Logan stopped the rental car at the back of the Planchet house. He'd left Texas early that morning, impatient to get back. His sense of anticipation had grown sharper with each mile that brought him closer to Little Rock. The sight of the dark green turrets gave him a sense of homecoming, although he'd only been in Arkansas for a few weeks.

Glancing at the rooftop of the cottage, he wondered where Tory was at this moment. That lady had quite a bit of explaining to do, he decided, getting out of the car and pulling his duffle bag out of the back seat. His hand automatically went to the letter in his pocket, making him take the back steps two at a time, anxious to find out where he could locate Tory.

Following the sound of voices, he walked directly to the dining room. He was stunned at the sight that greeted him. For a chilling moment he thought something had happened to Preston, but relaxed as he remembered his phone conversation with Babs last night.

Tory was the first one to notice him standing in the doorway, but she didn't say a word. Her dark eyes gleamed with amusement as she looked from him back to the others seated at the table. As usual the Planchets managed to provide the unexpected.

"Come on, Enid, there's absolutely nothing wrong with these suspenders," T.L. protested and hooked his thumbs under them, pulling them out for better inspection. He looked down with pride at the golden American eagles with their inch-wide wingspans. "The boys gave me these beauties for my birthday last year."

"T.L., you can't use beauty in the same sentence with those birds," Enid returned with disdain, but her smile took any sting out of the words. She turned to the other women for support. "Tory, Arnette, you tell him—Logan."

He was amazed at the uncharacteristic sight of his mother blushing. She seemed flustered at the sight of him. Logan couldn't remember another occasion when his mother hadn't been in complete control, the model of perfect behavior.

"Mother, I didn't know you were coming to visit," he said stiffly before nodding to others. T.L. returned his greeting with a smile. While Arnette insisted that he sit down and have something to eat, Tory refused to meet his gaze. She was very interested in the mound of mashed potatoes on her plate. Suddenly he felt like an outsider, awkward and uncomfortable.

"Come on and sit down, boy. You got here just in time for cholesterol Sunday," T.L. declared, waving Logan into a chair next to his mother. "I let Arnette have her way the rest of the month, but I demand some old-fashioned southern cooking once a month. No one can top Arnette's fried chicken and mashed potatoes. And her milk gravy just melts in your mouth."

At the mention of milk gravy, Logan looked across the table at Tory. She hadn't been able to resist either. He tried to read her expression, but the laughter he expected wasn't there. She gave nothing away. Did she really mean what she'd written? Could she really want to throw away everything that was between them?

Damn, if she wasn't the most frustrating woman he'd ever met. She made love like an angel, making him ache for more, but she had this nasty habit of disappearing when he was ready for a serious discussion. He'd had it. Tory Planchet was going to have to listen to him this time.

"How do you like Arkansas so far, Mother?" His tone was sharper than he intended. Nothing could be accomplished with Tory until they had some time alone, so he might as well deal with his surprise visitor. He was still trying to understand the laughing conversation he'd witnessed.

"It's been very pleasant. Did you enjoy Texas?" she answered in the prim voice he'd known all his life.

"Texas was interesting," he began, but hesitated at a sound from across the table. He was surprised to find Tory glaring at him.

What had he done wrong this time? Unfortunately, Arnette returned from the kitchen with his plate, and the moment was lost.

"Did you see Preston and Babs before you came down?" he continued after thanking Arnette. A polite conversation with his mother might help him get back his feeling of normalcy. "Babs didn't mention anything about your trip when I talked to her last night."

"I didn't actually mention it to them. Your uncle is doing fine. His new medicine seems to be doing him a world of good," Enid explained. Logan was fascinated that she was fidgeting with her silverware. That was an infraction that always sent him to his room.

"I hate to interrupt this warm reunion, but I need to

get back to the shop," Tory announced. She got to her feet abruptly. There was a militant set to her shoulders as she glanced at Logan. "Enid, do you still want to come along to see the shop? I won't be staying too long since Abby came in today as well."

"Yes, I think I will. Logan's probably tired from his trip." She almost jumped out of her seat at the invitation. Then for a moment she hesitated. "Is that all right with you, Logan?"

"Whatever you want to do, Mother," he returned, still trying to figure out what was going on around him. Why was Tory furious? It was as incomprehensible as his mother's attack of nerves. Thankfully, Arnette and T.L. were behaving normally, or he'd wonder if he'd entered the *Twilight Zone*.

The knock sounded on her front door at nine o'clock. Tory had been bracing herself for Logan's arrival all evening. She was dreading the confrontation, especially after his disgusting behavior at lunch. His cool treatment of his mother proved that she'd been right. Her wishful thinking had only fostered false hopes.

Tonight she'd get Logan Herrington out of her life once and for all. She pulled a face as she walked to the door, trying to remember how many times she'd come to that conclusion since their first meeting.

"Enid!" Logan's mother was the last person she expected to see when she opened the door.

"I'm not disturbing you, am I? If it's not a good time, I can talk to you later." Her anxious expression told Tory that she couldn't send her away.

"Come in."

"What a lovely room. Did you decorate it yourself?"

"Yes, I did, with a little help from an artist friend." Tory was uncertain about what to do next. The older woman was talking in the same monotone she'd used at lunch with Logan. When in doubt, eat, was Arnette's motto. "Can I get you something to drink? I was just having a cup of tea."

"That would be nice."

Tory returned from the kitchen a few minutes later with a tray ladened with a fresh pot of tea, lemon sponge cakes, and macaroons. Although she had an active imagination, she couldn't fathom why Logan's mother was there. Enid was standing by the fireplace, looking at the jumble of knickknacks that Tory had spread across the mantle.

"This fan is beautiful."

Tory set the tray down on the coffee table and was glad the silk fan gave her something to say. "Thank you. It's an heirloom that's always handed down to the oldest daughter, or in my case the only one. It was the groom's gift to an early Planchet bride, a *filles de la cassette*, New Orleans version of mail-order brides in the seventeen hundreds."

"Never make snap judgments," Enid murmured and sat down on the couch next to Tory. She accepted her cup of tea, but held the cup and saucer in her lap. "That's what I wanted to talk to you about, poor judgment. Your family's been in this country almost as long as the Herringtons and the Macombs, and you aren't the barefoot hillbillies I imagined. I came to apologize to you."

"Apologize to me?" Tory didn't try to hide her surprise. As far as she was concerned the only one who needed to apologize was Logan. His abrupt treatment of his mother today had been disgraceful.

"I behaved very badly when I arrived, and your family has treated me with nothing but kindness. I'm never very comfortable with strangers. In fact, they scare me to death. When I get nervous, I always manage to do and say the wrong thing and give the wrong impression,'' Enid explained. Her fingers played over the single strand of pearls around her neck. ''My grandmother was a true Victorian, and she helped my mother raise me. I was always told never to let anyone ever know what I was thinking or feeling, to pretend to have the emotions of a statue. I raised Logan the same way.''

''Cake?'' Tory held out the plate for lack of anything else to do or say. Why was Enid telling her this?

Enid took a sip of tea, almost as if it would give her courage to continue her speech. She took a deep breath and raised her chin. ''This is probably none of my business, especially since I came here to get him away from what I thought were horrible people. How do you feel about my son?''

Tory could only stare at the other woman. Was Enid here to ask her intentions toward Logan? This was revenge for the night she'd left Logan in the kitchen with T.L. She did the only thing that made sense, she picked up a lemon sponge cake and took a huge bite out of it.

''No, don't answer that last question,'' Enid told her. Setting her cup and saucer on the tray, she got up and began pacing the room. ''I think you'd be very good for Logan. You'd give him balance. He needs someone to break through his reserve.'' She paused for a moment, as if considering her next words, then gave a snort of disgust. ''Oh, this would have been so much easier if I was in my dowager war paint. There's something about jewels and furs that gives one a sense of authority.''

Tory almost choked on her second bite of cake. If only Logan could hear his mother tonight. Maybe she was dreaming, but if she was, she didn't want to wake up until Enid finished what she was saying. This was better than any of T.L.'s performances.

"Tory, have I made an absolute fool of myself by coming here?"

The vulnerable look on the older woman's face was something that Tory would remember for the rest of her life. "No, Enid. I'm very flattered that you think I would be good enough for your son."

"You're probably better than he deserves," his mother said dryly, relaxing under Tory's smile. "What I really want is his happiness. Much as I hate to admit it, my brother-in-law was right to get Logan out of Boston for a new perspective. I'm sure his behavior this afternoon was a reaction to my being here. I can't believe that he's resisted the charm of your family. There's something about you Planchets that puts a spell on people. T.L. is a true original."

"You aren't the first person to say that," Tory agreed, wondering about the effect that a Herrington seemed to have on a certain member of her family. Her life had been utter chaos since Logan set foot in Arkansas.

"I don't think I'll mention this little chat to Logan. What do you think?" Enid asked with a calculated look.

"That might be a good idea," Tory agreed, careful not to give away her feelings on the matter. So far, she'd managed to stay fairly neutral. "Would you like some more tea?"

"No, I think I've imposed on you long enough tonight. I have a few things to think over, mostly getting up enough courage to discuss my change of heart about Arkansas with Logan."

"You could start by asking him about the night we took my small niece and nephew to a Disney movie," Tory suggested as she walked her guest to the door. Enid's eyebrows almost reached her hairline at the comment. "I think he's still trying to get the grape drink and licorice stains out of his clothes."

Enid couldn't contain her laughter at Tory's smug smile. She leaned over and kissed her on the cheek. "Victoria Planchet, you are a gem."

Tory leaned back against the door after Enid left, hugging her arms tightly around her waist. Enid's visit had rekindled the tiny spark of hope once more. Was she crazy to think that they might have a future together after all?

Yes, she was going to take the chance. She'd been acting like a fool, a coward, creating more problems than were necessary just to remain independent. How valuable was her independence, if she didn't have the man she loved? Logan was arrogant and demanding, but so was she. Hadn't she been playing the autocrat herself during the last few weeks—demanding that he pass her tests, conform to her rules? He'd met every challenge and passed with flying colors.

Enid's apology echoed in Tory's mind. She realized she was a victim of her own snap judgments, just as Abby had implied the day of the Ferguson party. She'd fought her attraction to Logan without really knowing why. Deep inside she knew that he would change her life, ask for sacrifices that she hadn't been willing to make. She hadn't been willing to compromise, selfishly wanting everything to be on her terms.

Well, if Enid had enough courage to come and apologize to a relative stranger, she could face Logan and demand to know what type of relationship he wanted. Would he be willing to listen after the tests she put him through? She wasn't sure, but she had to try. She'd show him that southerners didn't always procrastinate. This lady could recognize a problem and take care of it.

Her hand was on the doorknob before she remembered that Logan wasn't home. She almost screamed in frustration. He'd gone out with Trevor tonight. She'd passed them at the gate earlier. It served her right, she decided, giving the door an impatient kick to relieve her frustration. After all the time she'd wasted, she would have to wait until tomorrow.

"Damn," Logan muttered and slammed the receiver down. The sound of plastic hitting metal echoed around the kitchen. Tory was right, he wasn't a morning person. But why didn't she have more than one telephone line at the store? This was the same mess he'd gone through before going to Texas. The woman just didn't stay in one place long enough.

"Is there a problem, son?"

He hadn't heard T.L. come into the kitchen while he was trying to get through to Bill of Fare. "That's the third time I've been cut off."

"An important call?"

Logan wasn't fooled by T.L.'s angelic look. He decided he wouldn't make the older man drag the information out of him. "I was trying to call your daughter. So far, she hasn't been there, or another call has come in and I get cut off. She needs more than one line."

"She's having another line installed next week. There wasn't time before the opening to get it set up," T.L. explained, leaning against the counter. He fished in his pocket for a minute and pulled out a small pearl handled knife. After he opened the blade, he began cleaning his fingernails, making it look perfectly normal while dressed in a suit. "Are you thinking about marrying my little girl?"

Logan watched the older man for a minute, wondering if he really wanted to get mixed up with this family for life. If he'd learned anything in Arkansas, it was how to play the Planchet game. Pulling out a chair from the table next to him, he turned it around and straddled it. He rested his arms along the back as he watched T.L.

"Trevor does a much better job of intimidation with a steak knife."

The older man looked up, grinning from ear to ear. "I know, but my number is coming up in the betting pool."

"You're betting on this? Of course, you are. Why did I bother to ask?" Logan couldn't help but laugh at the entire situation. "Who's in the pool?"

"Let's see," he pretended to consider the matter, silently counting on his fingers. "There's Trevor, Curtiss—Sanders refused because it wasn't dignified— Arnette, my secretary, my driver, and your mother kicked in this morning. And if Tory ever finds out about this, we're all dead meat."

"My mother?" He couldn't believe it. Apparently the Planchet magic had worked overtime. He was sure that his mother had come to Arkansas to drag him home, but she hadn't said a word about it to him. In fact, she hadn't said very much to him since he'd returned from Texas. This morning she'd gone off with Arnette on some excursion.

"Enid doesn't have much faith in you. She says it's going to take another two weeks for you to get your act together."

"Who has today?" Damned if he was going to let his friends and relatives make money on his lack of progress.

T.L. pulled a sheet of paper out of his vest pocket and ran his finger down the list. "Nobody. I'm betting on Wednesday."

"Don't count on it," Logan grunted and got to his feet.

"Hey, where are you going?" T.L. called after him as he headed for the back door.

"I think I'll go order something from Bill of Fare. I've developed quite an appetite," he answered, pushing the screen door open with the palm of his hand.

"Logan."

There was something in T.L.'s voice that made him stop at the top of the steps.

"Remember one thing when you're dealing with Tory. She's used to getting her own way. She's an independent little soul, but she can be reasoned with on occasion."

Logan nodded his understanding and bounded down the steps. T.L. knew his daughter well. He was more than willing to reason with Tory, find some sort of compromise, if he could just get the woman to stand still long enough to talk to her.

He drove to Park Plaza Mall and found a parking space in record time. If she wasn't at the shop now, she'd be back soon, and he'd be waiting for her. Tory Planchet was going to marry him, if he had to carry her down the aisle kicking and screaming. Now all he had to do was find out where her shop was in the three-level glass structure.

By the time he found the stain-glassed entrance to Bill of Fare, Logan had slowed his pace. His determination was modified by common sense. Every time he pushed too hard, Tory lost her temper. If he'd learned anything over the past few weeks, he'd learned that the lady didn't like to be told what to do. She'd also tried to teach him how to do things the southern way. And that was probably going to be her downfall.

The small dining area of the shop was filled with people eating lunch, and there was a line at the marble counter across the back. The only familiar face he saw was Abby Bush. When he caught her eyes, she waved at him and pointed in the back, behind the wooden, swinging doors. But she shook her head at his gesture to go back. A minute later Tory backed out the door with two food-laden rattan baskets in her hands.

He tried to intercept her as she took the basket to a table along the side wall, but he couldn't get around the people waiting in line before she went back in the kitchen.

"Hey, mister, take a number."

Without bothering to answer the man, Logan worked his way to the back of the shop. Tory would have to come out again. She did, five minutes later, walking right past him. He leaned against the counter, waiting for her come back, but enjoying watching her at work. Typically, she took time to talk to her customers.

He came to a decision by the time she came back.

"Excuse me, ma'am, I'm from the health department," he murmured so only she could hear him.

Tory stopped abruptly, blinking up at him in surprise. "Logan, what are you doing here?"

"I wasn't having any luck on the phone, so I decided to really reach out and touch someone." He matched his words by running his finger down her cheek. The expression on her face was a mixture of confusion and anticipation that gave him the courage for what he was about to do. "Apparently I came at a bad time."

"Tory, it's the laundry on the phone," Abby called from behind them, holding up the telephone.

"I can't really talk right now," Tory started to explain, seeming reluctant to leave him. He stopped her by placing his finger against her lips.

"That's all right. I just came over to tell you something I forgot to mention before I went to Texas. I love you." He smiled in satisfaction. For once, he'd managed to surprise a Planchet. "Are you going to stop running away now?"

"Tory, if you don't answer him in about five minutes, I'm quitting," Abby said impatiently from behind the counter. "You'll never be able to handle this crowd with only two people."

"Go away, Abby," Tory and Logan ordered together, but Tory didn't wait for her friend to leave. A smile lit up her face. "I love you, Logan."

"Good, I'll see you at home tonight," he returned, taking time to give her a quick kiss before walking out of the shop, whistling under his breath. He carried the stunned look on Tory's face with him as he executed the rest of his plan. She might not know it, but she was going to be given the full southern treatment.

Tory watched him walk out the door and wondered if she'd dreamed the whole episode. The silly grin on Abby's face seemed to verify that it had happened. She didn't have to worry for very long. If it was a dream, it was still going on.

Fifteen minutes later a package was delivered to Ms. Planchet from Mr. Herrington. Inside was a filigreed, heart-shaped locket purchased at the jewelry store three doors away from Bill of Fare. She soon discovered exactly how Logan spent his afternoon, working his way through the stores at the mall.

The Godiva chocolate roses came an hour after the necklace. At three o'clock she received a porcelain music box that was covered with hearts and cupids. By four o'clock, she didn't know what to expect, certainly not diamond earrings. He outdid himself at five, leaving Abby speechless and wiping the fatuous smile off her face that had been driving Tory crazy all afternoon.

With one look at the label, she tried to open the box in the privacy of her office, but Abby wouldn't be put off. Neither woman had seen anything as exquisite as the mostly lace and satin apricot colored teddy.

She was still a little dazed by the whole afternoon as she walked toward the cottage at six o'clock. Logan loved her, but where was he? The packages were accompanied by notes that simply said, "With love, Logan." The only thing she could think to do was come back to the cottage. His gifts had arrived on the hour, was he planning something else now?

Still caught up in her thoughts, Tory almost tripped over the shoe that was just inside the front door. She didn't remember leaving anything in the hallway. Taking a closer look, she realized that it was a man's shoe, and it belonged to someone she knew. Carefully putting her packages on the hall stand, she closed the door and turned on the light. The shoe was just the beginning.

Its mate was a few feet away, next to a pair of dark socks. Following the trail, she found a navy blue shirt at the end of the hall. A pair of jeans was lying just inside her bedroom door. His cotton briefs were between the door and the bed. Tory decided she liked this gift better than any of the others.

"Hi, have a nice day at work?" Logan asked from where he reclined on the bed with only a towel wrapped around his waist. "Why don't you slip into something more comfortable than your catering uniform and join me?"

Leaning against the door jamb, she matched his lazy smile. "Did you have something specific in mind?"

"I'm kind of partial to apricot colored lace. It's a taste I've developed since coming to Arkansas," he answered, linking his fingers behind his head.

She wasn't sure how long she could continue to play the game. He looked absolutely wonderful. "I think I have just the thing. Any other suggestions?"

"A friend of mine's been teaching me about relaxing

and relieving stress. I think you might want to take a nice, hot shower while I open the champagne." He inclined his head toward the nightstand where a magnum rested in a silver bucket.

"Not a bad idea, I'll be right back." She hurried back to the hall to retrieve her gifts, fumbling with her tie and the buttons on her vest as she went. Logan hadn't moved when she got back to the bedroom.

"Do you need any help?" he asked hopefully, watching with interest as she took off the top layer of her clothes. He groaned in disappointment when she stopped at her slip.

"Have the champagne ready in about ten minutes."

She was out of the shower in three minutes, but took time to freshen her makeup. The teddy fit her perfectly, slipping luxuriantly over her flushed skin. The man was incredible. She checked her appearance in the mirror as she dabbed jasmine scent at her elbows and knees. The necklace and earrings were the perfect accents.

She opened the door with a flourish, but the sight of Logan down on one knee stopped her on the threshold. "What are you doing?"

"Don't laugh at me, woman. I'm trying to do this right," he said with a show of dignity, grabbing at the towel that was trying to obey the law of gravity. "Come over here, so I can get this done in the proper southern style."

She moved toward him, her smile disappearing as she stopped in front of him. Butterflies were careening around her stomach. Suddenly she felt very nervous. He took her left hand in his and raised it to his lips.

"Victoria Camille Planchet, I humbly request your hand in marriage. This ring is a symbol of my undying love and devotion." His voice was a rough whisper of sound as he slipped a sapphire ring on her finger. "I need you in my life to temper my horrible Yankee ways and keep me from turning back into a preppie android.''

"Will you marry me? I promise to let you talk when we're out in public together, and you can wear shoes when you're pregnant. But I can't promise that I'll let you out of my sight for a minute until we've been married for two or three years, maybe longer."

Tory blinked back the tears that threatened to spill onto her cheeks in spite of his nonsense. She couldn't stand the pleading look in his eyes as he waited for her answer, clutching his towel with his right hand. Kneeling in front of him on the floor, she cupped his face in her palms. She leaned into his chest as she answered him with a kiss, sighing against his parted lips as his arms closed around her.

Reluctantly she pulled back, searching his face, trying to memorize his expression at that moment. "Although the thought of corrupting a Yankee for a lifetime is tempting, I'll only accept on one condition," she said softly, trailing a kiss over his chin. Tracing her lips over his jaw, she worked her way slowly back to the corner of his mouth. She could feel the beginning of his smile beneath her lips as he remembered their bargaining at Milt and Myrna's.

"What's the condition?"

Tilting her head back, she feathered her fingers through his hair. He had a wary look in his eyes, but his hands were moving with wicked intent over her bare back. "Don't ever act that humble again. It just doesn't suit you. Arrogance in some men is incredibly sexy, occasionally."

"Do you know that you are probably the most contradictory woman in the entire world?" he challenged, but kept her from answering with a searing kiss. It was a pledge of his love, a promise of a beautiful, fulfilling life.

"Hey, you're crying." Logan pulled back in surprise, tracing his finger down her damp cheek. "What is it, love?"

"I've just realized that I almost lost you by being so stubborn," she managed, trying to sniff delicately. "All my fine speeches about marriage making women idiots. I wasn't doing a very good job being single."

"Neither of us were at our best, love. We just didn't know that we'd both come out winners if we'd just compromise," he said comfortingly, dabbing at her tears with the end of his towel. "We were both used to getting our own way all the time."

"You were a quicker study than I was," Tory returned, luxuriating in the feel of his skin under her hands as she ran them over his shoulders. "I was still trying to get up the courage to face you again after writing that terrible letter."

"Reading that had to be one of the worst moments of my life. You'd done your usual disappearing act, and I had to be in Texas." He punished her by raining kisses over her face. "I don't remember anything about that trip except wanting to get back here as fast as I could."

"Logan?" She traced her finger over his collarbone and down the center of his chest, her eyes following the movement of her hand.

"Mmmmm?"

"Do you think we could continue this somewhere a little more comfortable? I'm not sure how much longer my knees are going to hold out." Leaning to the side, she inspected the floor to the side and behind him. "And you're going to catch cold in a very interesting place, since your towel seems to have slipped."

He tried to look thoughtful, but his gaze strayed to where his fingers were toying the thin strap of her teddy. "Does this mean I have permission to rip this delightful garment off your enticing body?"

"Is that any way to treat your investment?"

Logan didn't bother tó answer. He surged to his feet, taking her with him. In a flash of movement, he had them on the bed, pressing Tory into the mattress with the weight of his body. Propping himself up on his elbows, he caged her between his arms. "You're still overdressed."

"I'm sure a little Yankee ingenuity will take care of that," she returned and reached up to pull his head down to kissing distance. He didn't need any further encouragement.

All the teasing was forgotten as his mouth claimed her lips. The desire that had been shimmering beneath the surface, blossomed into life. Logan seemed determined to taste every portion of her body, trailing kisses from her neck to the valley between her breasts. She arched into him, impatient to ease the ache that was beginning to build inside her.

She gloried in the feel of his body pressing against hers, running her hands down his arms to his waist. Impatiently, she grasped his hips, pressing herself into the heat of his desire. The touch of his lips against her bare breast forced a moan of delight from her throat. She hadn't been aware of his clever fingers pulling the satin and lace from her body. Twisting beneath him, she murmured his name over and over as he pulled the garment free and tossed it over the side of the bed.

He couldn't resist her pleas. His legs pressed hers apart, settling himself in the feminine valley. With a slow, measured movement he entered her inner warmth. Raising his head, he watched her expression as he moved to complete their union. Neither of them moved, savoring the moment of commitment between them.

The tension was building, growing stronger. Logan began to move slowly, his tempo increasing with each movement. She wrapped her legs around his hips to deepen the thrust of his body, straining to reach some unknown goal. He rewarded her efforts by bending to tease the taut peaks of her breasts with his mouth. Crying out his name, she could feel herself spinning out of control.

Clinging to Logan, she tried to control the sensations, but it was too late. She was soaring toward completion, delicate tremors moving through her that suddenly transmitted themselves to the man holding her. Together they scaled the ultimate height of their passion and love.

The recovery was slow. Tory cradled Logan in her arms, wondering if she'd ever be able to move again. She savored the weight of his satiated body, stroking her hands over the damp skin of his back. He rubbed his head against her shoulder in response.

"Now that I have you at my mercy, I have another proposition for you," he murmured against the soft skin of her neck.

"What's that, sweetheart?" she asked lazily, brushing his hair back over his ear before running her hand over his shoulder. "Ouch. Why did you pinch me?"

Logan levered himself onto his elbow, but bent to kiss the wound he'd inflicted. "I needed to make sure I had your attention. This is important."

"All right," Tory said petulantly, but she had trouble keeping her lips from curving into a smile. She sat up, leaning back against the headboard and folded her hands primly beneath her breasts. When Logan's eyes seemed to stray, she asked, "Now who isn't paying attention?"

He quickly pulled the sheet over their bodies, covering any further distraction for both of them. Plumping up the pillow, he leaned back as well, pulling Tory into his arms. She went willingly, snuggling her head into the crook of his shoulder.

"So, what's this proposition?"

"It has to do with Boston," he said hesitantly. When she didn't respond, he continued, "I think the best solution is six months in Boston and six months in Little Rock."

His voice seemed strained. Tory sat up to see his expression.

"If that's what you want. Did you think I'd refuse?"

"I wasn't sure how you'd react to being carried off to a den of Yankees." He continued to watch her closely, seeming suspicious of her acquiescence.

Draping herself over his chest, she pressed her lips to his in a fleeting kiss. "I'm sure there'll be some consolation for my sacrifice."

"That can be arranged," he agreed, smiling against her lips.

"See, we can compromise when we put our minds to it," she murmured, exploring the line of his jaw. "If Proserpina could manage it, so can I."

"Proserpina?" Logan drew back suspiciously. "What does mythology have to do with living in Boston?"

"When Pluto kidnapped her, he fed her a pomegranate," Tory explained, resting her chin in the center of his chest. She continued her story with a grin. "She was forced to spend six months of the year above ground with the humans, and six months in Pluto's kingdom of He—"

Her words were cut off as Logan flipped her onto her back, pressing her into the mattress. He stopped her laughter with a fierce kiss. "I'm the one who ate the sausage biscuits, which are probably better than pomegranates any day. So, who's going to be spending six months where?"

"Winter in Arkansas and summer in Massachusetts. We'll arm wrestle over the other seasons," she promised before linking her arms around his neck.

"Are you sure, Tory? I want this to work."

Tory looked up into his earnest face, her eyes glowing with love and confidence. "This is an equal partnership with both of us working together. We're two parts of a whole. Besides, just think of all those Yankees I can corrupt."

"From now on this is the only Yankee you're going to practice your southern wiles on," Logan growled.

"Yes, dear," Tory promised, knowing she never had to worry about losing her independence again. She had something much better, a marriage based on mutual need, love, and understanding. Together they could do anything.